Arthur Conan Doyle

The Horror of the Heights

[ze słownikiem]

Arthur Conan Doyle

The Horror of the Heights

[ze słownikiem]

Groza na wysokości

Z PODRĘCZNYM SŁOWNIKIEM ANGIELSKO-POLSKIM

Ruda Śląska 2016

Wydawnictwo:

[ze słownikiem], www.zeslownikiem.pl, www.readings.pl
Facebook.com/zeslownikiem

Prawa autorskie:

eVirtualis sp. z o.o., ul. Karola Goduli 36, 41-712 Ruda Śląska

Redakcja:

Joanna Barańska, Sandra Ogińska

Projekt okładki:

Jan Paluch

Druk i oprawa:

Drukarnia Wydawnicza im. W. L. Anczyca S.A.

Kontakt:

biuro@zeslownikiem.pl

ISBN:

978-83-65646-21-7

Ruda Śląska 2016

CONTENTS

Tekst poniższej publikacji zawiera oryginalną treść oraz pisownię bez adaptacji i skrótów.

THE HORROR OF THE HEIGHTS

The idea that the extraordinary **narrative** which has been called the Joyce-Armstrong Fragment is an **elaborate** practical joke **evolved** by some unknown person, **cursed** by a **perverted** and **sinister** sense of humour, has now been **abandoned** by all who have examined the matter. The most **macabre** and **imaginative** of **plotters** would **hesitate** before linking his **morbid fancies** with the **unquestioned** and tragic facts which **reinforce** the statement. Though the **assertions** contained in it are amazing and even **monstrous**, it is none the less forcing itself upon the general intelligence that they are true, and that we must **readjust** our ideas to the new situation. This world of ours appears to be **separated** by a slight and **precarious** margin of safety from a most **singular** and unexpected danger. I will **endeavour** in this narrative, which **reproduces** the original document in its necessarily somewhat **fragmentary** form, to lay before the reader the whole of the facts **up to date**, **prefacing** my statement by saying that, if there be any who doubt the narrative of Joyce-Armstrong, there can be no question at all as to the facts concerning **Lieutenant** Myrtle, R. N., and Mr. Hay Connor, who undoubtedly met their end in the manner described.

abandoned - (abandon) porzucić, opuszczać; opuszczony
assertions - (assertion) twierdzenie, domaganie się, zapewnienie
cursed - (curse) kląć, przeklinać; przeklęty
elaborate - rozwodzić się; złożony, misterny, wyszukany, opracowany
endeavour - starać się; próba, staranie
evolved - (evolve) opracować, ewoluować
fancies - (fancy) wydawać się, przewidywać sukces; upodobanie, urojenie
fragmentary - fragmentaryczny, oderwany, okruchowy
hesitate - wahać się, zawahać się
imaginative - obdarzony wyobraźnią, pomysłowy
lieutenant - porucznik
macabre - makabryczny
monstrous - potworny, ogromny, monstrualny
morbid - niezdrowy, chorobliwy, przesadny
narrative - narracja, relacja
perverted - (pervert) deprawować; zboczeniec; zboczony, wypaczony; przewrotny
plotters - (plotter) intrygant, ploter
precarious - niebezpieczny, niepewny
prefacing - (preface) poprzedzić przedmową: wstęp, przedmowa
readjust - poprawić, wyregulować, dostosować
reinforce - popierać, wzmocnić, umocnić, zwiększyć
reproduces - (reproduce) wykonać, reprodukować, rozmnażać się, powielać
separated - (separate) oddzielać; rozdzielony
singular - wybitny, szczególny, osobliwy, pojedynczy, niezwykły
sinister - złowieszczy, złowrogi
unquestioned - bezsprzeczny, niekwestionowany
up to date - aktualny, najświeższy

aero club - aeroklub
binocular - binokle, lornetka; dwuoczny, obuoczny
briar - fajka z korzenia wrzośca
canvas-backed - z płóciennym grzbietem
coherence - spójność, koherencja
conjectured - (conjecture) przypuszczenie, domysł; mniemany
deplorable - godny ubolewania, opłakany, żałosny
detachable - odpinany, ruchomy, do oderwania, zdejmowany
ditch - zerwać, puścić, porzucić, pozbyć, wymknąć, rozwalić; rów
fluttering - (flutter) zatrzepotać, pomachać, zamrugać, dygotać, powiewać; trzepot, szelest, kołatanie, drganie; dygotanie, trzepotanie
footpath - ścieżka, chodnik
hedge - wykręcić, wykręcać się; zabezpieczenie, żywopłot
hiatus - przerwa, luka
in turn - po kolei, w rezultacie, z kolei
labourer - (labour) praca, trud, siła robocza; pracownik fizyczny, robotnik
manuscript - rękopis
nettles - (nettle) parzyć; pokrzywa zwyczajna
note-book - notatnik
perceived - (perceive) odebrać w pewien sposób, postrzegać, spostrzec; postrzegane
picked up - (pick up) podnosić, odebrać, zabrać, nauczyć się
record - notować, nagrywać; rekord, nagranie
westward - na zachód; zachodni

The Joyce-Armstrong Fragment was found in the field which is called Lower Haycock, lying one mile to the **westward** of the village of Withyham, upon the Kent and Sussex border. It was on the 15th September last that an agricultural **labourer**, James Flynn, in the employment of Mathew Dodd, farmer, of the Chauntry Farm, Withyham, **perceived** a **briar** pipe lying near the **footpath** which skirts the **hedge** in Lower Haycock. A few paces farther on he **picked up** a pair of broken **binocular** glasses. Finally, among some **nettles** in the **ditch**, he caught sight of a flat, **canvas-backed** book, which proved to be a **note-book** with **detachable** leaves, some of which had come loose and were **fluttering** along the base of the hedge. These he collected, but some, including the first, were never recovered, and leave a **deplorable** **hiatus** in this all-important statement. The note-book was taken by the labourer to his master, who **in turn** showed it to Dr. J. H. Atherton, of Hartfield. This gentleman at once recognized the need for an expert examination, and the **manuscript** was forwarded to the **Aero Club** in London, where it now lies.

The first two pages of the manuscript are missing. There is also one torn away at the end of the narrative, though none of these affect the general **coherence** of the story. It is **conjectured** that the missing opening is concerned with the **record** of Mr. Joyce-

Armstrong's qualifications as an **aeronaut**, which can be gathered from other sources and are admitted to be **unsurpassed** among the air-pilots of England. For many years he has been looked upon as among the most daring and the most intellectual of flying men, a combination which has enabled him to both invent and test several new devices, including the common **gyroscopic attachment** which is known by his name. The main body of the manuscript is written **neatly in ink**, but the last few lines are in pencil and are so **ragged** as to be hardly **legible**—exactly, in fact, as they might be **expected** to appear if they were **scribbled** off **hurriedly** from the seat of a moving **aeroplane**. There are, it may be added, several **stains**, both on the last page and on the outside cover which have been **pronounced** by the Home Office experts to be blood—probably human and certainly **mammalian**. The fact that something closely **resembling** the organism of malaria was discovered in this blood, and that Joyce-Armstrong is known to have suffered from **intermittent fever**, is a remarkable example of the new weapons which modern science has placed in the hands of our **detectives**.

And now a word as to the **personality** of the author of this **epoch-making** statement. Joyce-Armstrong, according to the few **friends** who really knew something of the man, was a poet and a dreamer, as well as a **mechanic** and an **inventor**. He was a man of **considerable**

aeronaut - aeronauta
aeroplane - samolot
attachment - przywiązanie, więź, załącznik, nasadka
considerable - znaczny
detectives - (detective) detektyw
epoch-making - epokowy, przełomowy
expected - (expect) spodziewać się, oczekiwać; spodziewany
friends - (friend) przyjaciel, znajomy
gyroscopic - żyroskopowy
hurriedly - pośpiesznie
in ink - napisany piórem
intermittent fever - gorączka przerywana
inventor - wynalazca
legible - czytelny
mammalian - należący do gromady ssaków
mechanic - mechanik, rzemieślnik; mechaniczny
neatly - schludnie, starannie, porządnie
personality - osobowość, charakter, postać
pronounced - (pronounce) wymawiać, oświadczać, ogłaszać; wyraźny
ragged - (rag) nabijać się, dokuczać; szmata, gazeta; wystrzępiony, poszarpany, umęczony
resembling - (resemble) przypominać
scribbled - (scribble) nabazgrać, nagryzmolić
stains - (stain) poplamić; plama
unsurpassed - niezrównany

aeronautical - aeronautyczny
airmen - (airman) lotnik
air-pockets - dziura powietrzna
altitude - wysokość
ascents - (ascent) unoszenie się, jazda pod górę, podejście
configuration - konfiguracja, ustawienie
construction - budowa, konstrukcja
debate - zastanawiać się nad, rozważać; debata, dyskusja
dinner - obiad
eccentricity - ekscentryczność
encounter - napotykać, spotykać, natykać się, doświadczać, zmierzyć się; spotkanie, potyczka
enigmatic - zagadkowy, enigmatyczny
entirely - całkowicie
faulty - wadliwy, błędny
gathering - (gather) zebrać się, zbierać, wnioskować; zbieranie
habit - nawyk, zwyczaj
hangars - (hangar) hangar
limbs - (limb) kończyna, konar, człon
manifestation - oznaka, przejaw, objaw
mess - bałagan, nieporządek, mesa, kantyna
narrate - opowiadać; być narratorem
obliterated - (obliterate) zrównać z ziemią, usunąć, skasować, zatrzeć; zatarty
occasion - okazja, sposobność
opinions - (opinion) opinia, zdanie
permanent - stały, trwały
pray - modlić się, błagać, prosić
preserved - (preserve) ochraniać, zabezpieczać, zachować; zachowane
pursuit - pogoń, dążenie, pościg
retiring - (retire) przejść na emeryturę, kłaść się spać, wycofywać się, opuszczać; odchodzący na emeryturę, małomówny
shot-gun - strzelba
smile - uśmiechać się; uśmiech
started - (start) zacząć, startować, rozpocząć, zrywać się; początek, zryw, wzdrygnięcie; rozpoczęty

wealth, much of which he had spent in the **pursuit** of his **aeronautical** hobby. He had four private aeroplanes in his **hangars** near Devizes, and is said to have made no fewer than one hundred and seventy **ascents** in the course of last year. He was a **retiring** man with dark moods, in which he would avoid the society of his fellows. Captain Dangerfield, who knew him better than anyone, says that there were times when his **eccentricity** threatened to develop into something more serious. His **habit** of carrying a **shot-gun** with him in his aeroplane was one **manifestation** of it.

Another was the morbid effect which the fall of Lieutenant Myrtle had upon his mind. Myrtle, who was attempting the height record, fell from an **altitude** of something over thirty thousand feet. Horrible to **narrate**, his head was **entirely** **obliterated**, though his body and **limbs** **preserved** their **configuration**. At every **gathering** of **airmen**, Joyce-Armstrong, according to Dangerfield, would ask, with an **enigmatic** **smile**: "And where, **pray**, is Myrtle's head?"

On another **occasion** after **dinner**, at the **mess** of the Flying School on Salisbury Plain, he **started** a **debate** as to what will be the most **permanent** danger which airmen will have to **encounter**. Having listened to successive **opinions** as to **air-pockets**, **faulty** **construction**, and over-banking, he ended by

shrugging his **shoulders** and **refusing** to **put forward** his own views, though he gave the impression that they **differed** from any **advanced** by his companions.

It is worth remarking that after his own complete **disappearance** it was found that his private affairs were arranged with a **precision** which may show that he had a strong **premonition** of disaster. With these essential explanations I will now give the narrative exactly as it stands, beginning at page three of the **blood-soaked** note-book:

"Nevertheless, when I **dined** at **Rheims** with Coselli and Gustav Raymond I found that neither of them was aware of any particular danger in the higher layers of the atmosphere. I did not **actually** say what was in my thoughts, but I got so near to it that if they had any **corresponding** idea they **could not** have failed to **express** it. But then they are two empty, **vainglorious** fellows with no thought beyond seeing their silly names in the newspaper. It is interesting to note that neither of them had ever been much beyond the twenty-thousand-foot level. Of course, men have been higher than this both in balloons and in the **ascent** of mountains. It must be well above that point that the aeroplane enters the danger zone—always **presuming** that my premonitions are correct.

"**Aeroplaning** has been with us now for more than twenty years, and one might well ask: Why

actually - tak właściwie
advanced - (advance) rozwijać się, płacić z góry, posuwać się naprzód; postęp; zaawansowany
aeroplaning - lecieć samolotem; latanie
ascent - unoszenie się, jazda pod górę, podejście, wspinaczka
blood-soaked - nasiąknięty krwią
corresponding - odpowiedni, analogiczny, korespondencyjny
could not - nie móc, nie potrafić
differed - (differ) różnić się
dined - (dine) obiadować, jeść obiad
disappearance - zanik, zniknięcie
express - wyrażać; ekspresowy, szybki
precision - precyzja
premonition - przeczucie
presuming - (presume) sądzić, założyć, przyjmować, nadużywać
put forward - przesunąć wskazówkę do przodu, zmienić czas na późniejszy, przedstawić coś, wysuwać
refusing - (refuse) odmawiać; odpadki
Rheims - Reims
shoulders - (shoulder) ramię
shrugging - (shrug) wzruszyć; wzruszenie ramion; wzruszając ramionami
vainglorious - chełpliwy, próżny

accurately - dokładnie, wiernie, celnie
ample - pokaźny, obszerny, obfity
asthma - astma
attaining - (attain) zdobyć, osiągać
chanced - (chance) zaryzykować; szansa; przypadkowy
come down - spaść, schodzić, przechodzić
descend - zejść, zstąpić, schodzić, obniżać; upadek, staczanie się
devoured - (devour) pożreć, pochłonąć, niszczyć, pustoszyć; pożarty
discomfort - niewygoda
immeasurably - niezmiernie, ogromnie
impunity - bezkarność
inhabit - zamieszkiwać
peril - zagrożenie, niebezpieczeństwo
restricted - ograniczony, wyznaczony, poufny, tajny, dozwolony od 17 lat
undertaken - (undertake) podjać się

should this **peril** be only revealing itself in our day? The answer is obvious. In the old days of weak engines, when a hundred horse-power Gnome or Green was considered **ample** for every need, the flights were very **restricted**. Now that three hundred horse-power is the rule rather than the exception, visits to the upper layers have become easier and more common. Some of us can remember how, in our youth, Garros made a world-wide reputation by **attaining** nineteen thousand feet, and it was considered a remarkable achievement to fly over the Alps. Our standard now has been **immeasurably** raised, and there are twenty high flights for one in former years. Many of them have been **undertaken** with **impunity**. The thirty-thousand-foot level has been reached time after time with no **discomfort** beyond cold and **asthma**. What does this prove? A visitor might **descend** upon this planet a thousand times and never see a tiger. Yet tigers exist, and if he **chanced** to **come down** into a jungle he might be **devoured**. There are jungles of the upper air, and there are worse things than tigers which **inhabit** them. I believe in time they will map these jungles **accurately** out. Even at the present moment I could name two of them. One of them lies over the Pau-Biarritz district of France. Another is just over my head as I write here in my house in Wiltshire. I rather think there is a third in the Homburg-Wiesbaden district.

"It was the disappearance of the airmen that first set me thinking. Of course, everyone said that they had fallen into the sea, but that did not satisfy me at all. First, there was Verrier in France; his machine was found near **Bayonne**, but they never got his body. There was the case of Baxter also, who **vanished**, though his engine and some of the iron **fixings** were found in a wood in Leicestershire. In that case, Dr. Middleton, of Amesbury, who was watching the flight with a **telescope**, declares that just before the clouds **obscured** the view he saw the machine, which was at an enormous height, suddenly rise **perpendicularly** upwards in a succession of **jerks** in a manner that he would have thought to be impossible. That was the last seen of Baxter. There was a correspondence in the papers, but it never led to anything. There were several other similar cases, and then there was the death of Hay Connor. What a **cackle** there was about an **unsolved** mystery of the air, and what columns in the **halfpenny** papers, and yet how little was ever done to get to the bottom of the business! He **came down** in a tremendous **vol-plane** from an unknown height. He never **got off** his machine and died in his pilot's seat. Died of what? 'Heart **disease**,' said the doctors. Rubbish! Hay Connor's heart was as sound as mine is. What did Venables say? Venables was the only man who was at his side when he died. He said that he was **shivering** and looked like a man who

Bayonne - Bajonna
cackle - gdakać, zachichotać, zarechotać; gdakanie, trajkot, rechot
came down - (come down) spaść, schodzić, upadać na ziemię, uspokoić się, przemieszczać się, podróżować, obniżać się, lądować, przyjechać
fixings - (fix) naprawić, załatwić, przymocować, ustawiać; ustalenie, urządzenie
got off - (get off) wysiadać, wychodzić, zdejmować
halfpenny - półpensówka, pół pensa
heart disease - choroba serca
jerks - (jerk) szarpać, pchać; szarpnięcie
obscured - (obscure) przesłaniać, ukrywać; niejasny, niewyraźny
perpendicularly - prostopadle, pionowo
shivering - (shiver) zadrżeć, zatrząść się, roztrzaskać, dygotać; drżenie, dreszcze, ciarki
telescope - teleskop, luneta
unsolved - nierozwiązany, niewyjaśniony
vanished - (vanish) wyparować, zniknąć, pierzchnąć; znikający
vol-plane - lecicec lotem ślizgowym; lot ślizgowy

chaff - podkpiwać z kogoś; plewy, śmiecie
dangerous - niebezpieczny
flannel - flanela, myjka do twarzy
fright - strach, trwoga
frightened - (frighten) przestraszyć kogoś, przerazić kogoś; przerażony
grease - nasmarować, posmarować tłuszczem; smar, tłuszcz, łój, maź
inquest - dochodzenie
queer - dziwny; dziwnie
scared - (scare) wystraszyć, spłoszyć, bać się; strach, popłoch, panika; wystraszony, przerażony
slimy - oślizgły, mulisty, mazisty, lepki, oślizły, obleśny
slippers - (slipper) kapeć, pantofelek, pantofel
subside - ustępować, opadać

had been badly **scared**. 'Died of **fright**,' said Venables, but could not imagine what he was **frightened** about. Only said one word to Venables, which sounded like 'Monstrous.' They could make nothing of that at the **inquest**. But I could make something of it. Monsters! That was the last word of poor Harry Hay Connor. And he DID die of fright, just as Venables thought.

"And then there was Myrtle's head. Do you really believe—does anybody really believe—that a man's head could be driven clean into his body by the force of a fall? Well, perhaps it may be possible, but I, for one, have never believed that it was so with Myrtle. And the **grease** upon his clothes—'all **slimy** with grease,' said somebody at the inquest. **Queer** that nobody got thinking after that! I did—but, then, I had been thinking for a good long time. I've made three ascents—how Dangerfield used to **chaff** me about my shot-gun—but I've never been high enough. Now, with this new, light Paul Veroner machine and its one hundred and seventy-five Robur, I should easily touch the thirty thousand tomorrow. I'll have a shot at the record. Maybe I shall have a shot at something else as well. Of course, it's **dangerous**. If a fellow wants to avoid danger he had best keep out of flying altogether and **subside** finally into **flannel slippers** and a dressing-gown. But I'll visit the air-jungle tomorrow—and if there's anything there I shall know it. If I return, I'll find myself a bit of a **celebrity**. If I don't this note-book may explain what I am trying to do, and how I lost my life in doing it. But no **drivel** about accidents or mysteries, if YOU please.

"I chose my Paul Veroner **monoplane** for the job. There's nothing like a monoplane when real work is to be done. Beaumont found that out in very early days. For one thing it doesn't mind **damp**, and the **weather** looks as if we should be in the clouds all the time. It's a **bonny** little model and answers my hand like a **tender-mouthed** horse. The engine is a ten-cylinder **rotary** Robur working up to one hundred and seventy-five. It has all the modern **improvements**—**enclosed fuselage**, high-curved landing **skids**, **brakes**, gyroscopic **steadiers**, and three speeds, worked by an **alteration** of the angle of the planes upon the **Venetian-blind** principle. I took a shot-gun with me and a dozen **cartridges filled** with **buck-shot**. You should have seen the face of Perkins, my old mechanic, when I **directed** him to put them in. I was **dressed** like an **Arctic explorer**, with two **jerseys** under my **overalls**, thick **socks inside** my **padded boots**, a storm-**cap** with **flaps**, and my **talc goggles**. It was **stifling** outside the hangars, but I was going for the **summit** of the **Himalayas**, and had to **dress** for the part. Perkins knew there was something on and **implored** me to take him with me. Perhaps I should if I were using the **biplane**, but a monoplane is a one-man show—

alteration - przebudowa, zmiana, przemiana
arctic - arktyczny, polarny, lodowaty
biplane - dwupłatowiec
bonny - śliczny, urodziwy, powabny
boots - (boot) but, bagażnik
brakes - (brake) zahamować; hamulec
buck-shot - śrut
cap - czapka, czepek, kapiszon
cartridges - (cartridge) nabój, kaseta
celebrity - sława, znakomitość, sława; honorowy; z udziałem samych znakomitości
damp - wilgoć; wilgotny, chłodny, przybity, stłumiony
directed - (direct) kierować, zarządzać, skierować, reżyserować; ukierunkowany
dress - ubierać; sukienka, strój
dressed - (dress) ubierać; sukienka, strój; ubrany
drivel - ślinić się, bredzić; brednie
enclosed - (enclose) otoczyć, mieścić w sobie, załączyć; osłonięty, obudowany
explorer - badacz, eksplorator
filled - (fill) wypełniać, napełnić; wypełniony
flaps - (flap) trzepotać, migotać; klapka
fuselage - kadłub
goggles - (goggle) wybałuszyć; gogle, okulary pływackie, okulary ochronne
Himalayas - (Himalaya) Himalaje
implored - (implore) błagać, napraszać się
improvements - (improvement) poprawa, postęp, ulepszenie
inside - wewnątrz
jerseys - (jersey) sweter, dzianina, dżersej
monoplane - jednopłat, jednopłatowiec
mouthed - (mouth) usta
overalls - (overall) kitel, fartuch, kombinezon
padded - (pad) cicho stąpać, zawyżać; blok, bloczek, podkładka; wywatowany
rotary - rondo; obrotowy, rotacyjny
skids - (skid) wpaść, popędzać kogoś; poślizg, dźwignia
socks - (sock) skarpeta
steadiers - (steady) regularny, stały, jednostajny; mocniejszy
stifling - (stifle) dusić, udaremnić, tłumić, spowalniać; duszny
summit - szczyt, na szczycie
talc - talk
tender - czuły, delikatny, wrażliwy
venetian-blind - żaluzja
weather - pogoda

if you want to get the last foot of life out of it. Of course, I took an oxygen bag; the man who goes for the altitude record without one will either be **frozen** or **smothered**—or both.

"I had a good **look at** the planes, the **rudder-bar**, and the **elevating lever** before I **got in**. Everything was in order so far as I could see. Then I **switched on** my engine and found that she was running **sweetly**. When they let her go she rose almost at once upon the lowest speed. I **circled** my home field once or **twice** just to warm her up, and then with a wave to Perkins and the others, I **flattened out** my planes and put her on her highest. She **skimmed** like a **swallow** down wind for eight or ten miles until I turned her nose up a little and she began to **climb** in a great **spiral** for the **cloud-bank** above me. It's all-important to rise slowly and **adapt yourself** to the pressure as you go.

"It was a close, warm day for an **English** September, and there was the **hush** and **heaviness** of **impending** rain. Now and then there came sudden **puffs** of wind from the south-west—one of them so **gusty** and unexpected that it caught me **napping** and turned me half-round for an **instant**. I remember the time when **gusts** and **whirls** and air-pockets used to be things of danger—before we **learned** to put an **overmastering** power into our engines. Just as I reached the cloud-banks, with the **altimeter** marking three

adapt - dostosować, zaadaptować
altimeter - wysokościomierz, altymetr
circled - (circle) krążyć; okrąg, koło; zakreślony
climb - wspinać się; wspinaczka
cloud-bank - chmury nisko na horyzoncie
elevating - (elevate) wynieść, podnieść; mechanizm podniesienia
English - angielski
flattened out - (flatten out) rozpłaszczyć, spłaszczyć
frozen - zamarznięty, mrożony
got in - (get in) przychodzić, przyjeżdżać, wsiadać, wchodzić
gusts - (gust) podmuch, poryw
gusty - porywisty, wietrzny
heaviness - ciężkość, ogrom
hush - uciszyć, wyciszyć, uspokoić; cisza; cicho!
impending - nieuchronnie zbliżający się
instant - chwila, moment; nie wymagający gotowania, natychmiastowy; od razu
learned - (learn) uczyć się; nauczony, uczony
lever - dźwignia, lewar
look at - przyglądać się, patrzeć, spojrzeć na coś
napping - (nap) pękać, drzemać, kłapnąć zębami
overmastering - opanowanie
puffs - (puff) dyszeć, sapać, wypuścić dym, pierdnąć; dmuchnięcia, podmuchy, bufka
rudder-bar - drążek steru
skimmed - (skim) usuwać z powierzchni, musnąć, przebiegać; przebiec wzrokiem
smothered - (smother) udusić, zdławić, tłamsić, zarzucać, pokryć; zdławiony
spiral - wzrosnąć; spirala; spiralny
swallow - połknąć, przełknąć; jaskółka, łyk
sweetly - mile, słodko, ślicznie, gładko
switched on - (switch on) włączać
twice - dwa razy
whirls - (whirl) kręcić się, wirować, wiercić się; wir
yourself - siebie

thousand, down came the rain. My word, how it **poured**! It **drummed** upon my wings and **lashed** against my face, **blurring** my glasses so that I could hardly see. I **got down** on to a low speed, for it was **painful** to **travel** against it. As I got higher it became **hail**, and I had to turn **tail** to it. One of my cylinders was **out of action**—a **dirty plug**, I should imagine, but still I was rising steadily with **plenty** of power. After a bit the trouble passed, whatever it was, and I **heard** the full, deep-**throated purr**—the ten **singing** as one. That's where the beauty of our modern **silencers** comes in. We can at last control our engines by ear. How they **squeal** and **squeak** and **sob** when they are in trouble! All those **cries** for help were **wasted** in the old days, when every sound was **swallowed up** by the monstrous **racket** of the machine. If only the early **aviators** could **come back** to see the beauty and **perfection** of the **mechanism** which have been **bought** at the cost of their lives!

"About nine-thirty I was nearing the clouds. Down below me, all **blurred** and **shadowed** with rain, lay the vast **expanse** of Salisbury Plain. Half a dozen flying machines were doing **hackwork** at the thousand-foot level, looking like little black swallows against the green **background**. I **dare** say they were **wondering** what I was **doing up** in cloud-land. Suddenly a grey **curtain** drew across beneath me and the **wet** folds of **vapours** were **swirling** round my

aviators - (aviator) lotnik
background - pochodzenie, tło, kontrast
blurred - (blur) rozmazać; niewyraźna plama; nieostry, niewyraźny
blurring - (blur) rozmazać; zamazany
bought - (buy) kupować
come back - wracać
cries - (cry) wołać, płakać; okrzyk
curtain - zasłona, kurtyna, kotara
dare - odważyć się, ośmielić, mieć czelność
dirty - brudny
doing up - (do up) zapiąć, zasunąć
drummed - (drum) bębnić, zagrać na bębnie; bęben, bębenek, baryłka, beczka
expanse - przestrzeń, powierzchnia, bezmiar
got down - (get down) zasmucać, przygnębiać, zapisywać, schodzić
hackwork - chaltura
hail - grad
heard - (hear) słyszeć, usłyszeć; zasłyszany, usłyszany
lashed - (lash) bić, chłostać, mocować, umocować; rzęsa, bicz, bat
mechanism - mechanizm
out of action - niepracujący, wyłączony
painful - bolesny, przykry
perfection - doskonałość, perfekcja
plenty - obfitość; dużo
plug - wtyczka, zatyczka, korek, prymka
poured - (pour) nalewać, zalewać, lać
purr - mruczeć; warkot
racket - robić harmider; rakieta, rakietka, wrzawa
shadowed - (shadow) cień; ocieniony
silencers - (silencer) tłumik
singing - (sing) śpiewać; śpiew, śpiewanie, gwizdanie; rozśpiewany
sob - zaszlochać, łkać; szloch
squeak - piszczeć, kwiczeć, skrzypnąć, zgrzytać, popiskiwać; pisk
squeal - zawyć z bólu, zakwiczeć; kwik, pisk
swallowed up - (swallow up) wchłaniać
swirling - (swirl) kłębić się; wirowanie, kłębienie się, obracanie
tail - śledzić kogoś; ogon, kita, część końcowa, poła
throated - (throat) gardło; gardłowy
travel - podróżować, jechać; podróż
vapours - (vapour) mgła, para, opary
wasted - (waste) marnować
wet - zmoczyć; mokry
wondering - (wonder) zastanawiać się, zdumieć się; cud

face. It was **clammily** cold and **miserable**. But I was above the hail-storm, and that was something **gained**. The cloud was as dark and thick as a London **fog**. In my **anxiety** to get clear, I **cocked** her nose up until the **automatic** alarm-bell **rang**, and I actually began to **slide** backwards. My **sopped** and **dripping** wings had made me heavier than I thought, but **presently** I was in lighter cloud, and soon had cleared the first layer. There was a second—opal-coloured and **fleecy**—at a great height above my head, a white, **unbroken ceiling** above, and a dark, unbroken floor below, with the monoplane labouring upwards upon a vast spiral between them. It is **deadly lonely** in these cloud-**spaces**. Once a great flight of some small water-birds went past me, flying very **fast** to the westwards. The quick **whir** of their wings and their musical **cry** were **cheery** to my ear. I **fancy** that they were **teal**, but I am a **wretched zoologist**. Now that we humans have become birds we must really **learn** to know our **brethren by sight**.

"The wind down beneath me **whirled** and **swayed** the **broad** cloud-plain. Once a great **eddy** formed in it, a **whirlpool** of **vapour**, and through it, as down a **funnel**, I caught sight of the **distant** world. A large white biplane was passing at a vast **depth** beneath me. I fancy it was the morning **mail** service **betwixt** Bristol and London. Then the **drift swirled inwards** again and the great **solitude** was unbroken.

anxiety - niepokój
automatic - automatyczny
betwixt - ni owo, między
brethren - brać; bracia
broad - szeroki, wyraźny, ogólny
by sight - z widzenia
ceiling - sufit
cheery - radosny, wesoły
clammily - lepko, oślizgle, parnie
cocked - (cock) podnosić
cry - wołać, płakać, zapłakać, zawołać; okrzyk
deadly - śmiercionośny, śmiertelny
depth - głębokość, głębia, otchłań
distant - odległy, daleki
drift - podryfować, popłynąć z prądem, unieść; prąd, sens, znoszenie
dripping - (drip) przemoknięty, ociekający wodą
eddy - zawirować, zafalować; wir
fancy - wydawać się
fast - szybki
fleecy - wełniasty
fog - mgła
funnel - lejek
gained - (gain) osiągać, zdobywać, zyskiwać; zysk; uzyskany
inwards - do wewnątrz
learn - uczyć się
lonely - samotny
mail - wysyłać; poczta
miserable - przygnębiony, nieszczęśliwy, nędzny
presently - obecnie, niebawem
rang - (ring) dźwięczeć, dzwonić
slide - zsunąć się, poślizgnąć się; slajd, ramka, ślizganie się
solitude - samotność
sopped - (sop) rozmoczyć; rozmoczony kawałek chleba, symboliczny gest
spaces - (space) przestrzeń
swayed - (sway) chwiać się, kołysać, skłaniać się; wpływ, władza
swirled - (swirl) kłębić się, zamierzać; zawijas, wirowanie
teal - kolor niebieski z odcieniem zielonkawym, cyraneczka
unbroken - nieprzerwany
vapour - mgła, para, opary
whir - brzęczeć; brzęczenie
whirled - (whirl) kręcić się, wirować, wiercić się; wir; krótka podróż
whirlpool - wir
wretched - (wretch) nieszczęśnik, nikczemnik; lichy, godny pożałowania
zoologist - zoolog

"Just after ten I touched the lower edge of the upper cloud-**stratum**. It **consisted** of fine **diaphanous** vapour drifting **swiftly** from the westwards. The wind had been steadily rising all this time and it was now **blowing** a **sharp breeze**—twenty-eight an hour by my **gauge**. Already it was very cold, though my altimeter only marked nine thousand. The engines were working **beautifully**, and we went **droning** steadily upwards. The cloud-bank was thicker than I had expected, but at last it **thinned** out into a **golden mist** before me, and then in an instant I had shot out from it, and there was an **unclouded** sky and a **brilliant** sun above my head—all blue and **gold** above, all **shining** silver below, one vast, **glimmering** plain as far as my eyes could reach. It was a **quarter** past ten **o'clock**, and the **barograph** needle pointed to **twelve** thousand eight hundred. Up I went and up, my ears **concentrated** upon the deep **purring** of my motor, my eyes **busy** always with the watch, the **revolution indicator**, the petrol lever, and the oil **pump**. **No wonder** aviators are said to be a **fearless** race. With so many things to think of there is no time to trouble about **oneself**. About this time I noted how **unreliable** is the **compass** when above a certain height from earth. At **fifteen** thousand feet mine was pointing east and a point south. The sun and the wind gave me my true bearings.

"I had hoped to reach an **eternal stillness** in these high altitudes, but with every thousand

barograph - barograf
beautifully - pięknie
blowing - (blow) dmuchać, wywiać, wiać; cios, dmuchanie, niemile widziany gość, nieznajomy
breeze - bryza
brilliant - jasny, jaskrawy, znakomity, olśniewający
busy - zajęty
compass - otoczyć, knuć; kompas, zasięg, zakres, cyrkiel
concentrated - (concentrate) skoncentrować, skupić
consisted - (consist) składać się z czegoś
diaphanous - przezroczysty, przeświecający
droning - (drone) brzęczeć, buczeć, warczeć; brzęczenie, cedzenie przez zęby
eternal - wieczny, nieustanny
fearless - nieustraszony
fifteen - piętnaście
gauge - zmierzyć, policzyć, ocenić; grubość, przekrój, wskaźnik, miernik
glimmering - (glimmer) migotać; migotanie, iskra, płomyk, przebłysk
gold - złoto; złota
golden - złoty
indicator - wskazówka, oznaka, wskaźnik, kierunkowskaz
mist - zamglić; zamglenie, mgła
no wonder - nic dziwnego
o'clock - o godzinie
oneself - się; sobie, samemu; siebie; samotnie
pump - pompować; pompa
purring - (purr) mruczeć; warkot
quarter - apartament, kwatera, jedna czwarta, ćwiartka, kwadrans, dzielnica, część miasta
revolution - rewolucja, obrót
sharp - ostry, bystry
shining - (shine) świecić, błyszczeć, polerować
stillness - bezruch, spokój, cisza
stratum - warstwa
swiftly - prędko
thinned - (thin) przerzedzać; chudy, cieński, słaby
twelve - dwanaście
unclouded - bezchmurne
unreliable - niesolidny, niepewny, niemiarodajny

bravely - dzielnie
buffeting - (buffet) walić o, zwalić się na
calculations - (calculation) wyliczenie
cast - rzucać, odlewać, zesłać, układać; odlew, forma
conqueror - zdobywca, zwycięzca
conquest - podbój
cord - sznurek, tasiemka, przewód
creation - tworzenie, dzieło
devotion - poświęcenie
divine - odgadnąć; boski
expecting - (expect) spodziewać się
fastened - (fasten) przymocować
gale - wichura
glorious - wspaniały
groaned - (groan) jęczeć, skrzypnąć
harp - harfa
heroic - bohaterski, heroiczny
hook - zaczepiać, zainteresować; hak
humming - (hum) nucić, brzęczeć
impose - nałożyć, narzucić
joint - staw, udziec, złącze, spoina, knajpka; wspólny, złączony, ruchomy
leathern - skórzany
limitations - (limitation) ograniczenie, niedoskonałość, słabość
merely - zaledwie, jedynie, tylko
midday - południe; południowy
mistress - dama, kochanka, nauczycielka, guwernantka, pani domu, pani
momentarily - na chwilę, wkrótce
mortal - śmiertelnik; śmiertelny
paid - (pay) płacić, opłacać; płatny
parachute - spadochron
ready - gotowy
ring - dźwięczeć, dzwonić; kółko
rivet - nitować, przykuć; nit
scamped - (scamp) łobuz, przekręt
severe - poważny, ciężki, srogi, surowy
sheet - szot, arkusz, tafla, prześcieradło
skimming - (skim) prześlizgiwać się
slacken - zwalniać, poluźnić
snap - pękać; trzask, pstryknięcie
stays - (stay) gorset, linka, podpora
strings - (string) struna
strut - kroczyć dumnie; rozpórka
superior - przełożony; ponadprzeciętny, wybitny, lepszy
tack - przyczepić; gwóźdź z dużą główką
trembled - (tremble) zadrżeć, drżeć, trząść się
unselfish - niesamolubny, bezinteresowny
vibrating - (vibrate) wprawić, drgać, drżeć
was after - (be after) poszukiwać, gonić, ścigać

feet of ascent the **gale** grew stronger. My machine **groaned** and **trembled** in every **joint** and **rivet** as she faced it, and swept away like a **sheet** of paper when I banked her on the turn, **skimming** down wind at a greater pace, perhaps, than ever **mortal** man has moved. Yet I had always to turn again and **tack** up in the wind's eye, for it was not **merely** a height record that I **was after**. By all my **calculations** it was above little Wiltshire that my air-jungle lay, and all my labour might be lost if I struck the outer layers at some farther point.

"When I reached the nineteen-thousand-foot level, which was about **midday**, the wind was so **severe** that I looked with some anxiety to the **stays** of my wings, **expecting momentarily** to see them **snap** or **slacken**. I even **cast** loose the **parachute** behind me, and **fastened** its **hook** into the **ring** of my **leathern** belt, so as to be **ready** for the worst. Now was the time when a bit of **scamped** work by the mechanic is **paid** for by the life of the aeronaut. But she held together **bravely**. Every **cord** and **strut** was **humming** and **vibrating** like so many **harp-strings**, but it was **glorious** to see how, for all the beating and the **buffeting**, she was still the **conqueror** of Nature and the **mistress** of the sky. There is surely something **divine** in man himself that he should rise so **superior** to the **limitations** which **Creation** seemed to **impose**—rise, too, by such **unselfish**, **heroic** **devotion** as this air-**conquest** has shown. Talk of human **degeneration**! When has such a story as this been written in the **annals** of our race?

"These were the thoughts in my head as I climbed that monstrous, **inclined** plane with the wind sometimes beating in my face and sometimes **whistling** behind my ears, while the cloud-land beneath me fell away to such a **distance** that the folds and **hummocks** of silver had all **smoothed** out into one flat, shining plain. But suddenly I had a horrible and **unprecedented** experience. I have known before what it is to be in what our **neighbours** have called a **tourbillon**, but never on such a **scale** as this. That huge, sweeping **river** of wind of which I have **spoken** had, as it appears, whirlpools within it which were as monstrous as itself. Without a moment's **warning** I was **dragged** suddenly into the heart of one. I **spun** round for a minute or two with such **velocity** that I almost lost my **senses**, and then fell suddenly, left **wing foremost**, down the **vacuum** funnel in the centre. I **dropped** like a **stone**, and lost nearly a thousand feet. It was only my belt that kept me in my seat, and the **shock** and **breathlessness** left me **hanging** half-**insensible** over the side of the fuselage. But I am always **capable** of a **supreme** effort—it is my one great **merit** as an **aviator**. I was conscious that the **descent** was **slower**. The whirlpool was a **cone** rather than a funnel, and I had come to the **apex**. With a **terrific wrench**,

annals - (annal) kronika, rocznik
apex - wierzchołek
aviator - lotnik
breathlessness - zadyszka, brak tchu
capable - zdolny
cone - stożek, rożek, pachołek, wafelek z lodami
degeneration - pogorszenie się, degeneracja, zwyrodnienie
descent - opadać; zejście, schodzenie, pochodzenie, najazd, atak, opadanie, rodowód
distance - odległość
dragged - (drag) ciągnąć, przeszukać, przeciągnąć, wlec, wciągnąć; nudziarz
dropped - (drop) upuścić, zrzucić, opaść, przestać, porzucić
foremost - główny, przedni; na pozycji lidera; najpierw, czołowo
hanging - (hang) wisieć, wieszać, powiesić; kotara; wiszące, wywieszone
hummocks - (hummock) wzgórek, pagórek, spiętrzenie lodu
inclined - (incline) przechylić
insensible - nieprzytomny, niewrażliwy
merit - zasłużyć się; wartość, zaleta
neighbours - (neighbour) sąsiadować; sąsiad, bliźni
river - rzeka
scale - wdrapać się; skala, łuska; wagowy
senses - (sense) czuć, wyczuwać; odczucie, zmysł, sens, rozsądek, rozum
shock - zaszokować; szok, wstrząs
slower - (slow) powolny; powolniejszy
smoothed - (smooth) wygładzać; gładki; wygładzony
spoken - (speak) mówić, przemawiać; mówiony
spun - (spin) wirować, sięgać, prząść; bomba, rewelacja
stone - kamień
supreme - najwyższy, największa
terrific - olbrzymi, wielki, straszny
tourbillon - (franc.) wir, trąba powietrzna
unprecedented - bezprecedensowy, niespotykany
vacuum - odkurzyć; próżnia, pustka, odkurzacz
velocity - prędkość
warning - (warn) ostrzegać, upominać, uprzedzać; ostrzeżenie
whistling - (whistle) gwizdać, śmignąć; gwizdek, gwizd
wing - polecieć, poszybować; skrzydło
wrench - szarpnąć, wyrwać; klucz francuski, szarpnięcie

throwing my weight all to one side, I levelled my planes and brought her head away from the wind. In an instant I had shot out of the eddies and was skimming down the sky. Then, **shaken** but **victorious**, I turned her nose up and began once more my **steady grind** on the **upward** spiral. I took a large sweep to avoid the danger-spot of the whirlpool, and soon I was **safely** above it. Just after one o'clock I was twenty-one thousand feet above the sea-level. To my great **joy** I had **topped** the gale, and with every hundred feet of ascent the air grew stiller. On the other hand, it was very cold, and I was conscious of that **peculiar nausea** which **goes with rarefaction** of the air. For the first time I **unscrewed** the **mouth** of my oxygen bag and took an **occasional whiff** of the glorious gas. I could feel it running like a **cordial** through my **veins**, and I was **exhilarated** almost **to the point** of **drunkenness**. I **shouted** and sang as I **soared** upwards into the cold, still outer world.

"It is very clear to me that the **insensibility** which came upon Glaisher, and in a lesser degree upon Coxwell, when, in 1862, they **ascended** in a balloon to the height of thirty thousand feet, was **due** to the **extreme** speed with which a **perpendicular** ascent is made. Doing it at an easy **gradient** and **accustoming** oneself to the **lessened barometric** pressure by **slow** degrees, there are no such **dreadful symptoms**. At the same great height I found

accustoming - (accustom) przyzwyczaić
ascended - (ascend) wspiąć, wjechać, wznosić się
barometric - barometryczny
cordial - syrop owocowy, likier; serdeczny, szczery
dreadful - okropny, fatalny, straszny, potworny
drunkenness - pijaństwo
due - należny; z powodu
exhilarated - (exhilarate) upoić, wprawić
extreme - skrajny
goes with - (go with) pasować, towarzyszyć, dziać się jako skutek czegoś
gradient - pochyłość, stopień nachylenia, gradient
grind - siekać, ostrzyć, szlifować; harówka, zgrzytanie
insensibility - zamroczenie, niewrażliwość, obojętność
joy - radość
lessened - (lessen) zmniejszyć, złagodzić, obniżyć, przycichnąć; zmniejszony, osłabiony
mouth - usta
nausea - mdłości, nudności
occasional - okolicznościowy, sporadyczny
peculiar - dziwny, osobliwy, szczególny
perpendicular - prostopadły, pionowy
rarefaction - rozrzedzenie
safely - bezpiecznie
shaken - (shake) zatrząść, potrząsać, wstrząsać; wstrząs; wstrząśnięty
shouted - (shout) krzyczeć; krzyk, pokrzykiwania
slow - powolny
soared - (soar) unosić się, wzrosnąć, podskoczyć, gwałtownie wzrastać, szybować
steady - podtrzymać, podpierać; stały, zrównoważony, opanowany
symptoms - (symptom) objaw, przejaw
throwing - (throw) wyrzucić, rzucić, niedbale położyć; rzucanie
to the point - na temat, do rzeczy
topped - (top) przewyższać, przebijać; wierzchołek, szczyt, top, wierzch
unscrewed - (unscrew) odkręcać; odkręcony
upward - w górę, do góry; zwrócony ku górze
veins - (vein) żyła, nerw, ton, nuta
victorious - zwycięski
whiff - wciągać ustami; zapach, woń, zapowiedź, dmuchnięcie, zaciągnięcie się

that even without my oxygen **inhaler** I could **breathe** without **undue distress**. It was **bitterly** cold, however, and my **thermometer** was at zero, Fahrenheit. At one-thirty I was nearly seven miles above the surface of the earth, and still **ascending** steadily. I found, however, that the **rarefied** air was giving **markedly** less support to my planes, and that my angle of ascent had to be **considerably** lowered in **consequence**. It was already clear that even with my light weight and strong engine-power there was a point in front of me where I should be held. To **make matters worse**, one of my **sparking-plugs** was in trouble again and there was intermittent **misfiring** in the engine. My heart was **heavy** with the **fear** of **failure**.

"It was about that time that I had a most extraordinary experience. Something **whizzed** past me in a **trail** of smoke and exploded with a loud, hissing sound, **sending forth** a cloud of **steam**. For the instant I could not imagine what had **happened**. Then I remembered that the earth is for ever being **bombarded** by meteor stones, and would be hardly **inhabitable** were they not in nearly every case **turned to** vapour in the outer layers of the atmosphere. Here is a new danger for the high-altitude man, for two others passed me when I was nearing the forty-thousand-**foot mark**. I cannot doubt that at the edge of the earth's **envelope** the risk would be a very real one.

ascending - (ascend) wspiąć, wjechać, wznosić się
bitterly - przenikliwie, gorzko
bombarded - (bombard) zbombardować
breathe - oddychać, wydychać, szeptać
consequence - konsekwencja, znaczenie, waga
considerably - znacznie, w znacznym stopniu
distress - zmartwić; rozpacz, ból, niebezpieczeństwo
envelope - pokrywać; koperta, powłoka
failure - niepowodzenie
fear - bać się, obawiać się; strach
foot mark - stopa wysokości
forth - naprzód, dalej
happened - (happen) wydarzyć się, zdarzyć się; wydarzenie
heavy - ciężki
inhabitable - nadający się do zamieszkania
inhaler - inhalator
make matters worse - co gorsza, na domiar złego
markedly - wyraźnie
misfiring - (misfire) nie wypalić, nie zapalić
rarefied - rozrzedzony, ekskluzywny
sending - (send) wysyłać, posłać; wysłanie
sparking-plugs - świeca zapłonowa
steam - para; parowy
thermometer - termometr
trail - podążyć, snuć się, ciągnąć za sobą; szlak, smuga, ślad, trop
turned to - (turn to) zwracać się, skierować się, zmieniać się w coś, zmieniać się
undue - nadmierny, zbytni
whizzed - (whizz) brzęczeć, świszczeć, przebiec

airtract - ścieżka akrobatyczna
attained - (attain) zdobywać, osiągnąć; zdobyty, osiągnięty
attenuated - (attenuate) osłabić, złagodzić; rozrzedzony
bear - nosić, ścierpieć, wytrzymać, rodzić, znosić; niedźwiedź
capacity - pojemność, zdolność, stanowisko
careful - ostrożny, staranny
entered - (enter) wchodzić, wejść
guide - prowadzić, zaprowadzać, oprowadzać; przewodnik
hawk - jastrząb
heavens - (heaven) niebiosa, niebo
hunter - myśliwy, drapieżnik, koń do polowania
indication - oznaka, wskazówka, przejaw
least - najmniej
limit - ograniczać; limit
observation - obserwacja
physically - fizycznie
possibly - możliwie
searching - (search) poszukiwać; poszukiwanie; badawczy, dociekliwy, wnikliwy, dokładny
side-slip - ślizg
sluggish - niemrawy, spowolniony, wolny, wolno płynący
soaring - (soar) unosić się, wzrosnąć, podskoczyć; wznoszenie, latanie, zwyżka, rośnięcie
somewhere - gdzieś
strain - nadwyrężać, odsączać; odmiana, szczep, obciążenie, wysiłek
surroundings - (surround) otaczać; otoczenie, okolica
tilt - przechylać, przekrzywiać, przechylać się; nachylenie, plandeka
wished - (wish) życzyć sobie, chcieć, życzyć

"My barograph needle marked forty-one thousand three hundred when I became aware that I could go no farther. **Physically**, the **strain** was not as yet greater than I could **bear** but my machine had reached its **limit**. The **attenuated** air gave no firm support to the wings, and the **least tilt** developed into **side-slip**, while she seemed **sluggish** on her controls. **Possibly**, had the engine been at its best, another thousand feet might have been within our **capacity**, but it was still misfiring, and two out of the ten cylinders appeared to be out of action. If I had not already reached the zone for which I was **searching** then I should never see it upon this journey. But was it not possible that I had **attained** it? **Soaring** in circles like a monstrous **hawk** upon the forty-thousand-foot level I let the monoplane **guide** herself, and with my Mannheim glass I made a **careful observation** of my **surroundings**. The **heavens** were perfectly clear; there was no **indication** of those dangers which I had imagined.

"I have said that I was soaring in circles. It struck me suddenly that I would do well to take a wider sweep and open up a new **airtract**. If the **hunter entered** an earth-jungle he would drive through it if he **wished** to find his game. My reasoning had led me to believe that the air-jungle which I had imagined lay **somewhere** over Wiltshire. This should be to the south and west of me. I took my bearings from the sun, for the compass was **hopeless** and no **trace** of earth was to be seen—nothing but the distant, silver cloud-plain. However, I got my **direction** as best I might and kept her head **straight** to the mark. I **reckoned** that my petrol **supply** would not last for more than another hour **or so**, but I could **afford** to use it to the last **drop**, since a single **magnificent** vol-plane could at any time take me to the earth.

"Suddenly I was aware of something new. The air in front of me had lost its **crystal clearness**. It was full of long, ragged **wisps** of something which I can only **compare** to very fine **cigarette smoke**. It **hung about** in **wreaths** and **coils**, turning and **twisting** slowly in the **sunlight**. As the monoplane shot through it, I was aware of a **faint taste** of oil upon my **lips**, and there was a **greasy scum** upon the **woodwork** of the machine. Some **infinitely** fine **organic** matter appeared to be **suspended** in the atmosphere. There was no life there. It was **inchoate** and **diffuse**, **extending** for many **square acres** and then **fringing** off into the **void**. No, it was not life. But might it not be the **remains** of life? Above all, might it not be the food of life, of monstrous life, even as the **humble** grease of the ocean is the food for the **mighty whale**? The thought was in my mind when my eyes looked upwards and I saw the most wonderful vision that ever man has seen. Can I hope to **convey** it to you even as I saw it myself last Thursday?

afford - pozwalać, mieć na coś pieniądze, oferować
cigarette smoke - dym papierosowy
clearness - przejrzystość, bezbarwność
coils - (coil) zwinąć, owinąć, wić się; zwój, krąg, lok, spirala
compare - porównać
convey - przewozić, przekazywać, wyrażać
crystal - kryształ; krystaliczny
diffuse - rozproszony, rozmyty, rozwlekły
direction - wskazówka, instrukcja
drop - kropla
extending - (extend) rozciąganie się
faint - zasłabnąć, zemdleć; omdlenie; słaby
fringing - (fringe) okalać, ciągnąć się wzdłuż
greasy - tłusty, przetłuszczający się, zatłuszczony
hopeless - beznadziejny
humble - skromny, pokorny
hung about - (hang about) kręcić się, pałętać się
inchoate - nieokreślony, niesprecyzowany
infinitely - nieskończenie
lips - (lip) warga, brzeg, krawędź
magnificent - wspaniały
mighty - potężny
or so - mniej więcej, około
organic - organiczny, naturalny, jednolity
reckoned - (reckon) myśleć, sądzić, przypuszczać, liczyć
remains - (remain) pozostałości
scum - szumowina, męt, kożuch, osad brudu
square acres - akr kwadratowy
straight - prosty; prosto
sunlight - światło słoneczne
supply - dostarczać, zaopatrywać; dostawa, zapas
suspended - (suspend) przerywać, zawieszać; zawieszony, wstrzymany
taste - smakować, skosztować; smak, gust
trace - namierzać, wyśledzić, śledzić; ślad, uprząż
twisting - (twist) skręcić, kręcić; skręcony, kręty
void - próżnia, otchłań; pusty
whale - wieloryb
wisps - (wisp) kosmyk, wiązka, smuga
woodwork - stolarka, stolarki, stolarstwa, konstrukcja drewniana
wreaths - (wreath) wieniec, kłęby

amidst - wsród, z powodu
argosies - (argosy) galeon
attuned - (attune) być wyczulonym na coś
average - średni; średnia, przeciętny
conceive - wyobrażać sobie, stworzyć
curvature - skrzywienie, krzywizna
dainty - przysmak; delikatny, drobny
delicacy - delikatność, subtelność
depended - (depend) zależeć, polegać
dignity - godność, powaga, szacunek
dome - kopuła, nakryty kopułą
drooping - (droop) zwiędnąć; zwisający
fabric - materia, konstrukcja, tkanka
fairy - wróżka, bajka; czarodziejski
finest - (fine) grzywna; cienki, delikatny, lekki, pogodny, dobry; najlepszy
fleet - flota, park, konwój; szybki, rączy
fragile - kruchy, delikatny, słaby
gorgeous - wspaniały
iridescence - mienienie się tęczowymi barwami, opalizacja
jelly-fish - meduza
judge - osądzać; sędzia
look after - opiekować się, pilnować, szukać
majority - większość, pełnoletność
noiseless - bezgłośny
outline - przedstawić w zarysie; kontur
pale - blednąć; blady
perfect - idealny
prevailing - (prevail) dominujący
pulsated - (pulsate) pulsujący
pure - czysty, niewinny, całkowity
regular - regularny
reminded - (remind) przypominać
rhythm - rytm
sails - (sail) żagiel
shades - (shade) odcień, cień
shaped - (shape) kształtować; kształt, forma, w kształcie
shimmered - (shimmer) mienić się, drgać; migotanie, blask
soap-bubble - bańka mydlana
squadron - eskadra, szwadron, dywizjon
stately - okazały, majestatyczny
strange - dziwny
tentacles - (tentacle) macka, czułek, włosek
tenuous - cienki, wątły, słaby, naciągnięty, subtelny, luźny
texture - konsystencja, struktura
tints - (tint) odcień, szampon koloryzujący, koloryzować
top - wierzchołek, szczyt, top
veined - (vein) żyła, nerw, ton, nuta; żylasty, żyłkowany

"**Conceive** a **jelly-fish** such as **sails** in our summer seas, bell-**shaped** and of enormous size—far larger, I should **judge**, than the **dome** of St. Paul's. It was of a light pink colour **veined** with a delicate green, but the whole huge **fabric** so **tenuous** that it was but a **fairy outline** against the dark blue sky. It **pulsated** with a delicate and **regular rhythm**. From it there **depended** two long, **drooping**, green **tentacles**, which swayed slowly backwards and forwards. This **gorgeous** vision passed gently with **noiseless dignity** over my head, as light and **fragile** as a **soap-bubble**, and drifted upon its **stately** way.

"I had half-turned my monoplane, that I might **look after** this beautiful creature, when, in a moment, I found myself **amidst** a **perfect fleet** of them, of all sizes, but none so large as the first. Some were quite small, but the **majority** about as big as an **average** balloon, and with much the same **curvature** at the **top**. There was in them a **delicacy** of **texture** and colouring which **reminded** me of the **finest** Venetian glass. **Pale shades** of pink and green were the **prevailing tints**, but all had a lovely **iridescence** where the sun **shimmered** through their **dainty** forms. Some hundreds of them drifted past me, a wonderful fairy **squadron** of **strange** unknown **argosies** of the sky—creatures whose forms and substance were so **attuned** to these **pure** heights that one could not conceive anything so delicate within **actual** sight or sound of earth.

"But soon my attention was drawn to a new **phenomenon**—the **serpents** of the outer air. These were long, **thin**, **fantastic** coils of vapour-like material, which turned and **twisted** with great speed, flying round and round at such a pace that the eyes could hardly follow them. Some of these **ghost-like** creatures were twenty or thirty feet long, but it was difficult to tell their **girth**, for their outline was so **hazy** that it seemed to **fade away** into the air around them. These air-**snakes** were of a very light grey or smoke colour, with some darker lines within, which gave the impression of a **definite** organism. One of them **whisked** past my very face, and I was conscious of a cold, **clammy** **contact**, but their **composition** was so unsubstantial that I could not **connect** them with any thought of **physical** danger, any more than the beautiful bell-like creatures which had **preceded** them. There was no more **solidity** in their **frames** than in the floating **spume** from a broken wave.

"But a more **terrible** experience was in **store** for me. Floating **downwards** from a great height there came a **purplish** **patch** of vapour, small as I saw it first, but **rapidly** **enlarging** as it **approached** me, until it appeared to be hundreds of square feet in size. Though **fashioned** of some **transparent**, jelly-like

actual - rzeczywisty
approached - (approach) zbliżać się; podejście; zbliżony, przybliżony
clammy - lepki, oślizły, parny
composition - skład, struktura, kompozycja, utwór
connect - połączyć, złączyć, przyłączyć
contact - kontaktować się; kontakt
definite - określony, sprecyzowany, konkretny
downwards - w dół, do dołu, skierowany w dół; zniżkowy
enlarging - (enlarge) powiększyć, zwiększyć, rozwinąć, wzrosnąć, rozszerzyć
fade away - zanikać
fantastic - fantastyczny; fantastycznie
fashioned - (fashion) kształtować, modelować; moda, styl; stylowy
frames - (frame) obramowywać, okalać, formułować; postura, rama; ramowy
ghost-like - przypominający ducha
girth - obwód, obwód w pasie
hazy - mglisty, zamglony, niewyraźny
patch - łatać; łata, przepaska, grządka, bruzda, skrawek
phenomenon - zjawisko, fenomen
physical - fizyczny
preceded - (precede) poprzedzać, iść przed; poprzedzone
purplish - o zabarwieniu purpurowym, fioletowawy
rapidly - szybko
serpents - (serpent) wąż
snakes - (snake) wąż
solidity - twardość, solidność, trwałość, zasadność
spume - pienić się; piana
store - magazynować, przechowywać, gromadzić; sklep, zapasy; duża ilość
terrible - straszny, okropny
thin - przerzedzać; chudy, cieńki, słaby
transparent - przezroczysty, klarowny
twisted - (twist) skręcić; skręcony
whisked - (whisk) ubijać, szybko zabrać, przeszyć powietrze, śmignąć; trzepaczka do jajek; pacnięty

substance, it was none the less of **much more** definite outline and solid **consistence** than anything which I had seen before. There were more traces, too, of a physical **organization**, especially two vast, **shadowy**, **circular plates** upon either side, which may have been eyes, and a perfectly solid white **projection** between them which was as curved and **cruel** as the **beak** of a **vulture**.

"The whole aspect of this monster was **formidable** and threatening, and it kept **changing** its colour from a very light **mauve** to a dark, **angry** purple so thick that it cast a **shadow** as it drifted between my monoplane and the sun. On the upper **curve** of its huge body there were three great projections which I can only describe as enormous bubbles, and I was **convinced** as I **looked at** them that they were **charged** with some **extremely** light gas which **served** to **buoy up** the **misshapen** and **semi-solid** mass in the rarefied air. The creature moved swiftly along, keeping pace easily with the monoplane, and for twenty miles or more it formed my horrible **escort**, **hovering** over me like a **bird of prey** which is **waiting** to **pounce**. Its method of **progression**—done so swiftly that it was not easy to follow—was to **throw out** a long, **glutinous streamer** in front of it, which in turn seemed to draw forward the rest of the **writhing** body. So **elastic** and **gelatinous** was it that never for two successive minutes was it the same **shape**, and yet each

angry - zły
beak - dziób
bird of prey - ptak drapieżny
buoy up - unosić się na wodzie
changing - (change) zmieniać; zmiana, wymiana pieniędzy
charged - (charge) oskarżać, policzyć, nakazać; koszt, opłata, oskarżenie, atak; naładowany, napięty
circular - kolisty, okrągły
consistence - konsekwencja, zgodność
convinced - (convince) przekonać, namówić, przekonywać; przekonany
cruel - okrutny
curve - zakrzywić, wyginać; krzywa, wygięcie
elastic - elastyczny, rozciągliwy
escort - eskortować; eskorta
extremely - niezwykle
formidable - potężny, ogromny, bardzo trudny
gelatinous - galaretowaty
glutinous - kleisty, lepki
hovering - (hover) wisieć, unosić się w powietrzu, wahać się
looked at - (look at) przyglądać się, patrzeć
mauve - fioletoworóżowy
misshapen - zniekształcony
much more - dużo bardziej
organization - organizacja
plates - (plate) talerz, tabliczka
pounce - skakać, rzucić się
progression - rozwój, postępy, poprawa
projection - przewidywanie, wizja, projekcja, wypustka, występ
semi-solid - pół stały
served - (serve) podawać, serwować, służyć, obsługiwać
shadow - cień; ocieniony
shadowy - zaciemniony, ciemny
shape - kształtować; kształt, forma, w kształcie
streamer - serpentyna, wstęga
throw out - wyrzucić, pozbyć się, odrzucić
vulture - sęp
waiting - (wait) czekać, oczekiwać; czekanie; oczekujący, czychający
writhing - (writhe) zwinąć, skręcić; wijący się

change made it more threatening and **loathsome** than the last.

"I knew that it **meant mischief**. Every purple **flush** of its **hideous** body told me so. The **vague**, **goggling eyes** which were turned always upon me were cold and **merciless** in their **viscid hatred**. I **dipped** the nose of my monoplane downwards to **escape** it. As I did so, as quick as a **flash** there shot out a long **tentacle** from this mass of floating **blubber**, and it fell as light and **sinuous** as a **whip-lash** across the front of my machine. There was a loud **hiss** as it lay for a moment across the **hot** engine, and it whisked itself into the air again, while the huge, flat body drew itself together as if in sudden **pain**. I dipped to a vol-**pique**, but again a tentacle fell over the monoplane and was **shorn** off by the **propeller** as easily as it might have **cut** through a smoke **wreath**. A long, **gliding**, **sticky**, **serpent-like coil** came from behind and caught me round the **waist**, **dragging** me out of the fuselage. I **tore** at it, my **fingers sinking into** the **smooth**, **glue-like** surface, and for an instant I **disengaged** myself, but only to be caught round the **boot** by another coil, which gave me a **jerk** that tilted me almost on to my back.

"As I fell over I **blazed** off both **barrels** of my gun, though, indeed, it was like **attacking** an **elephant** with a **pea-shooter** to imagine that any human **weapon** could **cripple** that mighty

attacking - (attack) atakować; atak
barrels - (barrel) lufa, korpus
blazed - (blaze) wybuch, nacięcie
blubber - beczeć; tłuszcz, sadełko
boot - but, bagażnik
coil - lok, spirala
cripple - okaleczyć, sparaliżować; kaleka
cut - ciąć, rozciąć
dipped - (dip) zanurzać, zniżyć
disengaged - (disengage) rozłączyć, zaprzestać, uwolnić się, uwolnić; wolny
dragging - (drag) ciągnąć
elephant - słoń
escape - uciekać, unikać, umykać; ucieczka, uciekanie
fingers - (finger) palec
flash - migać, błyskać, przemykać; błysk
flush – poczerwienieć; rumieniec
gliding - (glide) ślizgać się, sunąć, szybować; szybownictwo
glue-like - przypominający klej
goggling eyes - (goggle eyes) z wybałuszonymi oczami
hatred - nienawiść
hideous - szkaradny, ohydny
hiss - syknąć; syk, syknięcie, szum
hot - gorąco
jerk - szarpać, pchać; szarpnięcie, nagły ruch
lash - bić, chłostać, mocować, umocować; rzęsa, bicz, bat
loathsome - wstrętny
meant - (mean) oznaczać
merciless - bezlitosny
mischief - krzywda, nieszczęście
pain - boleć; trudy, ból
pea-shooter - broń o małym kalibrze, rurka do strzelania grochem
pique - wzbudzić; uraza, irytacja
propeller - śmigło, śruba napędowa
serpent-like - przypominający węża
shorn - (shear) ostrzyc, wystrzyc
sinking into - (sink into) zatopić w czymś coś
sinuous - kręty, wijący się
smooth - wygładzać; gładki
sticky - lepki, kleisty, ciekawski, wścibski, paskudny
tentacle - macka, czułek, włosek
tore - (tear) pędzić, rozdzierać, rwać
vague - mętny, niejednoznaczny, nieokreślony, niepewny, niejasny
viscid - lepki, zawiesisty
waist - talia, pas
weapon - broń
whip - smagnąć, ściągnąć, bat, bicz
wreath - wieniec, kłęby

bulk. And yet I **aimed** better than I knew, for, with a loud report, one of the great **blisters** upon the creature's back exploded with the **puncture** of the buck-shot. It was very clear that my **conjecture** was right, and that these vast, clear **bladders** were **distended** with some **lifting gas**, for in an instant the huge, cloud-like body turned **sideways**, writhing **desperately** to find its **balance**, while the white beak snapped and **gaped** in horrible **fury**. But already I had shot away on the **steepest glide** that I dared to attempt, my engine still full on, the flying propeller and the force of **gravity shooting** me downwards like an **aerolite**. Far behind me I saw a **dull**, purplish **smudge growing** swiftly smaller and merging into the blue sky behind it. I was **safe** out of the deadly jungle of the outer air.

"Once out of danger I **throttled** my engine, for nothing **tears** a machine to pieces quicker than **running on** full power from a height. It was a glorious, spiral vol-plane from nearly eight miles of altitude—first, to the level of the silver cloud-bank, then to that of the storm-cloud beneath it, and finally, in beating rain, to the surface of the earth. I saw the **Bristol Channel** beneath me as I **broke** from the clouds, but, having still some petrol in my **tank**, I got twenty miles **inland** before I found myself **stranded** in a field half a mile from the village of Ashcombe. There I got three **tins** of petrol from a passing motor-car, and at ten minutes past six that

aerolite - meteoryt kamienny
aimed - (aim) dążyć do, celować; cel
balance - balansować; saldo, równowaga
bladders - (bladder) pęcherz, pęcherzyk
blisters - (blister) spowodować powstanie pęcherzy, pokryć, łuszczyć się, złuszczyć; pęcherz, pęcherzyk
Bristol Channel - Kanał Bristolski
broke - (break) zepsuć się, przerwać, rozbić, połamać, złamać, pokonać; przerwa
bulk - ładunek, kolor; wielki rozmiar, hurtowy, masowy
conjecture - przypuszczenie, domysł
desperately - beznadziejnie, rozpaczliwie
distended - (distend) rozdąć, wydąć, rozciągnąć; spuchnięty, rozciągnięty
dull - nieciekawy, tępy, nudny, nijaki
fury - furia
gaped - (gape) gapić się, rozwierać się
glide - ślizgać, sunąć, szybować; ślizg, szybowanie
gravity - ciężkość, ciążenie, powaga, grawitacja
growing - (grow) rosnąć, wzrosnąć, rozwijać się, stawać się
inland - śródlądowy, leżący w głębi lądu, krajowy
lifting gas - gaz do podnoszenie np. hel
puncture - przebić, przekłuć, obalić, pęknąć; przebicie, dziura, nakłucie
running on - (run on) działać na coś, kontynuować
safe - bezpieczny
shooting - (shoot) strzelać, pędzić, wystrzelić, rzucać; pęd; spadający, przeszywający, kłujący
sideways - (sideway) bokami, bokiem; na boki, do boku, z ukosa
smudge - rozmazać; plama
steepest - (steep) namoczyć, pozwolić; stromy; najbardziej stromy
stranded - (strand) kosmyk; pozostawiony, unieruchomiony
tank - czołg, zbiornik, cysterna, basen, bak
tears - (tear) łzawić, pędzić, rozdzierać, szarpać się; rozdarcie, łza
throttled - (throttle) udusić, zdławić; przepustnica, zawór dławiący
tins - (tin) puszka, cyna, blacha

evening I **alighted** gently in my own home **meadow** at Devizes, after such a journey as no mortal upon earth has ever yet taken and **lived** to tell the tale. I have seen the beauty and I have seen the horror of the heights—and greater beauty or greater horror than that is not within the **ken** of man.

"And now it is my plan to go once again before I give my **results** to the world. My reason for this is that I must surely have something to show by way of **proof** before I lay such a tale before my fellow-men. It is true that others will soon follow and will **confirm** what I have said, and yet I should **wish** to carry **conviction** from the first. Those lovely **iridescent** bubbles of the air should not be **hard** to **capture**. They drift slowly upon their way, and the **swift** monoplane could **intercept** their **leisurely** course. It is likely enough that they would **dissolve** in the heavier layers of the atmosphere, and that some small **heap** of **amorphous** jelly might be all that I should bring to earth with me. And yet something there would surely be by which I could **substantiate** my story. Yes, I will go, even if I run a risk by doing so. These purple horrors would not seem to be **numerous**. It is **probable** that I shall not see one. If I do I shall **dive** at once. At the worst there is always the shot-gun and my knowledge of ..."

alighted - (alight) wysiąść, zsiąść, wylądować, siadać, spocząć; płonący, jasnego koloru
amorphous - amorficzny, bezpostaciowy, bezkształtny
capture - zdobyć, wziąć; zdobycie, schwytanie
confirm - potwierdzić, zatwierdzić
conviction - przekonanie, pewność
dissolve - rozpuścić, zniknąć, rozpłynąć; przenikanie
dive - zanurkować, spaść; skok do wody, nurkowanie, spadanie, lot nurkowy
hard - ciężko
heap - zwalić na kogoś coś, ułożyć, leżeć na kupie; sterta
intercept - zatrzymywać, przechwycić; punkt przecięcia prostej z osią współrzędnych
iridescent - mieniący się barwami, opalizujący
ken - (know) rozpoznać; znany
leisurely - powolny, spokojny, robiony w wolnym czasie; spokojnie, powolnie
lived - (live) żyć, mieszkać, zamieszkiwać; żywy
meadow - łąka
numerous - liczny
probable - prawdopodobny
proof - uodparniać; dowód
results - (result) wynikać; wynik
substantiate - poprzeć, potwierdzić
swift - jerzyk; szybki, błyskawiczny
wish - życzyć sobie, chcieć; życzenie

admit - przyjąć, przyznać
commend - pochwalić, polecić, powierzyć
disappeared - (disappear) znikać, zgubić się
dwell - zamieszkiwać, przebywać, rezydować; dom, mieszkanie, siedlisko
entirety - całość
fled - (flee) uciekać, umykać, frunąć
gradually - stopniowo, powoli
grim - ponury, zacięty, nędzny, okrutny
jeer - wyszydzić, wyśmiać; gwizdy, drwiny
nameless - bezimienny, nieokreślony
overtaken - dogonić; wyprzedzony, zaskakiwany
prefer - woleć, preferować
preserves - (preserve) ochraniać, zabezpieczać, zachować; konserwa, domena, specjalność
relics - (relic) relikt, pozostałość
sanity - zdrowie psychiczne, zdrowy rozsądek
shattered - (shatter) rozbijać, niszczyć; zrujnowany, roztrzaskany
straggling - (straggle) ociągać się, wlec się; rozproszony, rosnący w różnych kierunkach
terrors - (terror) terror
unfortunate - niefortunny, nieszczęśliwy
unfortunately - niestety
valued - (value) cenić, wyceniać; wartość; drogi, cenny; ceniony
victim - ofiara

Here a page of the manuscript is **unfortunately** missing. On the next page is written, in large, **straggling** writing:

"Forty-three thousand feet. I shall never see earth again. They are beneath me, three of them. God help me; it is a dreadful death to die!"

Such in its **entirety** is the Joyce-Armstrong Statement. Of the man nothing has since been seen. Pieces of his **shattered** monoplane have been picked up in the **preserves** of Mr. Budd-Lushington upon the borders of Kent and Sussex, within a few miles of the spot where the note-book was discovered. If the **unfortunate** aviator's theory is correct that this air-jungle, as he called it, existed only over the south-west of England, then it would seem that he had **fled** from it at the full speed of his monoplane, but had been **overtaken** and devoured by these horrible creatures at some spot in the outer atmosphere above the place where the **grim relics** were found. The picture of that monoplane skimming down the sky, with the **nameless terrors** flying as swiftly beneath it and cutting it off always from the earth while they **gradually** closed in upon their **victim**, is one upon which a man who **valued** his **sanity** would **prefer** not to **dwell**. There are many, as I am aware, who still **jeer** at the facts which I have here set down, but even they must **admit** that Joyce-Armstrong has **disappeared**, and I would **commend** to them his own words: "This note-book may explain what I am trying to do, and how I lost my life in doing it. But no drivel about accidents or mysteries, if YOU please."

Vocabulary of all words in this book

a jakiś, pewien
abandoned (abandon) porzucić, opuszczać; opuszczony
about o
above powyżej
accidents (accident) wypadek
according (accord) udzielić, wyświadczyć, zgadzać się, przyznać; porozumienie; według, zgodnie z
accurately dokładnie, wiernie, celnie
accustoming (accustom) przyzwyczaić
achievement osiągnięcie, dokonanie, zdobycie, odniesienie, zrealizowanie, realizacja
acres (acre) akr
across przez
action akcja
actual rzeczywisty
actually tak właściwie
adapt dostosować, zaadaptować
added (add) dodawać; dodany
admit przyjąć, przyznać
admitted (admit) przyjąć, przyznać
advanced (advance) rozwijać się, płacić z góry, posuwać się naprzód; postęp; zaawansowany
aero dotyczący powietrza lub latania
aero club aeroklub
aerolite meteoryt kamienny
aeronaut aeronauta
aeronautical aeronautyczny
aeroplane samolot
aeroplaning lecieć samolotem; latanie
affairs (affair) sprawa, wydarzenie, romans
affect oddziaływać, wzruszać, udawać
afford pozwalać, mieć na coś pieniądze, oferować
after po
again jeszcze raz
against przeciwko
agricultural rolniczy, rolny
aimed (aim) dążyć do, celować; cel
air powietrze
airmen (airman) lotnik
air-pockets dziura powietrzna
airtract ścieżka akrobatyczna
alarm alarmować, niepokoić; alarm, trwoga
alighted (alight) wysiąść, zsiąść, wylądować, siadać, spocząć; płonący, jasnego koloru
all wszystko, wszyscy
almost prawie
along wzdłuż
Alps Alpy
already już
also również
alteration przebudowa, zmiana, przemiana
altimeter wysokościomierz, altymetr
altitude wysokość
altogether całkowicie, razem
always zawsze
am (be) być, jestem
amazing (amaze) zadziwiać, zdumieć; niesamowity
amidst wsród, z powodu
among pośród
amorphous amorficzny, bezpostaciowy, bezkształtny
ample pokaźny, obszerny, obfity
an jakiś, pewien
and i
angle ustawiać pod kątem; kąt, punkt widzenia
angry zły
annals (annal) kronika, rocznik
another inny
answer odpowiedzieć, odebrać, odpowiadać, reagować; odpowiedź
anxiety niepokój
any jakikolwiek
anybody ktoś, nikt, ktokolwiek
anyone ktokolwiek
anything coś, cokolwiek, nic, byle co

apex wierzchołek
appear wydawać się, zjawić się, pojawiać się, wyglądać
appeared (appear) wydawać się, zjawić się, pojawiać się, wyglądać
appears (appear) wydawać się, zjawić się, pojawiać się, wyglądać
approached (approach) zbliżać się; podejście; zbliżony, przybliżony
arctic arktyczny, polarny, lodowaty
are (be) być; jesteś, jesteśmy, jesteście, są
argosies (argosy) galeon
around na około
arranged (arrange) organizować, ustalać, układać; ułożony
as tak jak
ascended (ascend) wspiąć, wjechać, wznosić się
ascending (ascend) wspiąć, wjechać, wznosić się
ascent unoszenie się, jazda pod górę, podejście, wspinaczka
ascents (ascent) unoszenie się, jazda pod górę, podejście
ask zapytać, pytać, prosić
aspect aspekt
assertions (assertion) twierdzenie, domaganie się, zapewnienie
asthma astma
at w
at heart w głębi duszy
atmosphere atmosfera
attachment przywiązanie, więź, załącznik, nasadka
attacking (attack) atakować; atak
attained (attain) zdobywać, osiągnąć; zdobyty, osiągnięty
attaining (attain) zdobyć, osiągać
attempt próbować, usiłować; próba
attention uwaga
attenuated (attenuate) osłabić, złagodzić; rozrzedzony
attuned (attune) być wyczulonym na coś
author autor
automatic automatyczny
average średni; średnia, przeciętny
aviator lotnik
aviators (aviator) lotnik
avoid zapobiegać, omijać, unikać
aware świadomy
away z dala
back cofać, wycofywać; plecy; tylny, wycofany, posiadający oparcie; z powrotem
backed (back) cofać, wycofywać; plecy; tylny, wycofany, posiadający oparcie; z powrotem; z powrotem
background pochodzenie, tło, kontrast
backwards (backward) opóźniony w rozwoju, zacofany; wspak, do tyłu, wstecz; tylny
badly źle, ciężko
bag zapakować, zdobywać; torba
balance balansować; saldo, równowaga
balloon spuchnąć; balon
balloons (balloon) spuchnąć; balon
bank bank, ławka, brzeg
bar zakazywać, zagradzać, zaryglować; bar, pręt, rygiel, drążek, pasek
barograph barograf
barometric barometryczny
barrels (barrel) beczkować; beczka, beczułka, baryłka, lufa, zbiorniczek, korpus
base bazować, opierać się, ugruntować; baza, podstawa
Bayonne Bajonna
be być
beak dziób
bear nosić, ścierpieć, wytrzymać, rodzić, znosić; niedźwiedź
bearings (bear) nosić, ścierpieć, wytrzymać, rodzić, znosić; postawa, łożysko, kierunek
beating (beat) pokonywać, bić, pobić; bijący
beautiful piękny
beautifully pięknie
beauty piękno, uroda, ślicznotka
became (become) stać się, zostać
become stać się, zostać
been (be) być

before przed
began (begin) zacząć, zapoczątkować; początek
beginning (begin) zacząć, zapoczątkować; początek; rozpoczęcie
behind za
being (be) być, będąc; istota, stworzenie
believe uwierzyć, wierzyć
believed (believe) uwierzyć, wierzyć
bell dzwon
below poniżej
below me (below sb) poniżej czyjejś godności
belt pędzić; pas, pasek, obszar, strefa
beneath pod
best (good) dobry; najlepszy
better (good) dobry; lepszy
between pomiędzy
betwixt ni owo, między
beyond poza, za, później niż, więcej
big duży
binocular binokle, lornetka; dwuoczny, obuoczny
biplane dwupłatowiec
bird ptak
bird of prey ptak drapieżny
birds (bird) ptak
bit kawałek, część, bit
bitterly przenikliwie, gorzko
black czarny
bladders (bladder) pęcherz, pęcherzyk
blazed (blaze) płonąć, palić się; ogień, płomień, pożar, wybuch, gwiazdka, strzałka, nacięcie
blind oślepić; zasłona, żaluzja; ślepy
blisters (blister) spowodować powstanie pęcherzy, pokryć, łuszczyć się, złuszczyć; pęcherz, pęcherzyk
blood krew
blood-soaked nasiąknięty krwią
blowing (blow) dmuchać, wywiać, wiać; cios, dmuchanie, niemile widziany gość, nieznajomy
blubber beczeć; tłuszcz, sadełko
blue niebieski
blurred (blur) rozmazać; niewyraźna plama; nieostry, niewyraźny
blurring (blur) rozmazać; niewyraźna plama; zamazany
body ciało
bombarded (bombard) zbombardować
bonny śliczny, urodziwy, powabny
book książka
boot but, bagażnik
boots (boot) but, bagażnik
border graniczyć; lamówka, granica
both obie
bottom dół, dno, sedno; dolny, najniższy
bought (buy) kupować
brakes (brake) zahamować; hamulec
bravely dzielnie
breathe oddychać, wydychać, szeptać
breathlessness zadyszka, brak tchu
breeze bryza
brethren brać; bracia
briar fajka z korzenia wrzośca
brilliant jasny, jaskrawy, znakomity, olśniewający
bring przynieść
Bristol Channel Kanał Bristolski
broad szeroki, wyraźny, ogólny
broke (break) zepsuć się, przerwać, rozbić, połamać, złamać, pokonać; przerwa
broken (break) zepsuć się, przerwać, rozbić, połamać; przerwa; złamany, spłukany, zrujnowany, przewany, rozbity, przerwany, poprzerywany, zepsuty
bubble pienić się, musować; pęcherzyk, bąbelek
buck dolec, sarna, młody byczek, najniższy w stopniu
buck-shot śrut
buffeting (buffet) walić o, zwalić się na; szturchanie, bufet, bar
bulk ładunek, kolor; wielki rozmiar, hurtowy, masowy
buoy podnieść; boja, pława
buoy up unosić się na

wodzie
business biznes, interesy
busy zajęty
but ale
by przez
by sight z widzenia
cackle gdakać, zachichotać, zarechotać; gdakanie, trajkot, rechot
calculations (calculation) wyliczenie, wyrachowanie
called (call) dzwonić, nazywać, wołać; nazwany
came (come) podchodzić, podejść, nadjeżdżać
came down (come down) spaść, schodzić, upadać na ziemię, uspokoić się, przemieszczać się, podróżować, obniżać się, lądować, przyjechać
can móc, mogą; puszka
cannot nie może, nie móc
canvas grube płótno, płótno z żagli; brezentowy
canvas-backed z płóciennym grzbietem
cap czapka, czepek, kapiszon
capable zdolny
capacity pojemność, zdolność, stanowisko
captain kapitan
capture zdobyć, wziąć; zdobycie, schwytanie
car samochód, wagon
careful ostrożny, staranny
carry nosić, dźwigać, przewozić; przewóz, transport
cartridges (cartridge) nabój, kaseta
case sprawa, przypadek
cases (case) sprawa, przypadek
cast rzucać, odlewać, zesłać, układać; odlew, forma
caught (catch) łapać, złapać, chwytać
ceiling sufit
celebrity sława, znakomitość, sława; honorowy; z udziałem samych znakomitości
centre umieścić, umieszczać na środku; centrum, środek, ośrodek
certain pewny
certainly na pewno
chaff podkpiwać z kogoś; plewy, śmiecie
chanced (chance) zaryzykować; szansa; przypadkowy
change zmieniać; zmiana, wymiana pieniędzy
changing (change) zmieniać; zmiana, wymiana pieniędzy
channel droga, kanał
charged (charge) oskarżać, policzyć, nakazać; koszt, opłata, oskarżenie, atak; naładowany, napięty
cheery radosny, wesoły
chose (choose) wybierać, postanowić
cigarette papieros
cigarette smoke dym papierosowy
circled (circle) krążyć; okrąg, koło; zakreślony
circles (circle) okrąg, koło
circular kolisty, okrągły
clammily lepko, oślizgle, parnie
clammy lepki, oślizły, parny
clean czyścić, sprzątać; czysty
clear czyścić, oczyszczać, sprzątać; usuwanie, odblokowanie; jasny, przezroczysty
clearness przejrzystość, bezbarwność
climb wspinać się; wspinaczka
clock zegar
close zamykać; koniec; blisko
closely blisko, z bliska; uważnie, dokładnie
clothes (clothe) ubierać, ubrać; ubranie, ubiór; odziany
cloud przyćmić; chmura, zachmurzenie
cloud-bank chmury nisko na horyzoncie
clouds (cloud) przyćmić; chmura
club tłuc pałką; klub, kij golfowy, maczuga, pałka, trefl
cocked (cock) podnosić, odciągać kurek strzelby, odwieść, obracać; kogut, kurek, przyjaciel, kapelusz dwurożny
coherence spójność, koherencja
coil zwinąć, owinąć, wić się; zwój, krąg, lok, spirala
coils (coil) zwinąć, owinąć, wić się; zwój, krąg, lok, spirala

cold zimno, przeziębienie
collected (collect) kolekcjonować, zbierać; skupiony
colour stroić się w cudze piórka; kolor, barwa, barwność, kolor skóry, rumieniec; kolorowy, barwny
columns (column) kolumna
combination połączenie
come podchodzić, podejść, nadjeżdżać, podjeżdżać; udawanie; przyszły, następny
come back wracać
come down spaść, schodzić, przechodzić
commend pochwalić, polecić, powierzyć
common pospolity
companions (companion) towarzysz
compare porównać
compass otoczyć, knuć; kompas, zasięg, zakres, cyrkiel
complete ukończyć, skończyć; kompletny
composition skład, struktura, kompozycja, utwór
conceive wyobrażać sobie, stworzyć
concentrated (concentrate) skoncentrować, skupić
concerned (concern) dotyczyć, martwić; zaangażowany, zaniepokojony
concerning (concern) dotyczyć, martwić; w odniesieniu do, dotyczący
cone stożek, rożek, pachołek, wafelek z lodami
configuration konfiguracja, ustawienie
confirm potwierdzić, zatwierdzić
conjecture przypuszczenie, domysł
conjectured (conjecture) przypuszczenie, domysł; mniemany
connect połączyć, złączyć, przyłączyć
conqueror zdobywca, zwycięzca
conquest podbój
conscious świadomy, zamierzony
consequence konsekwencja, znaczenie, waga
considerable znaczny
considerably znacznie, w znacznym stopniu
considered (consider) rozważać, rozpatrywać; przemyślany, rozważony
consisted (consist) składać się z czegoś
consistence konsekwencja, zgodność
construction budowa, konstrukcja
contact kontaktować się; kontakt
contained (contain) zawierać, pomieścić, powstrzymywać się
control kontrola
convey przewozić, przekazywać, wyrażać
conviction przekonanie, pewność
convinced (convince) przekonać, namówić, przekonywać; przekonany
cord sznurek, tasiemka, przewód, sztruks, linia
cordial syrop owocowy, likier; serdeczny, szczery
correct poprawiać, korygować; poprawny
correspondence korespondencja
corresponding odpowiedni, analogiczny, korespondencyjny
cost kosztować; koszt
could (can) móc, umieć, potrafić
could not nie móc, nie potrafić
course kurs
cover przykryć, nakryć, okryć; pokrywa, przykrycie, nakrycie, okładka
creation tworzenie, dzieło
creature stworzenie, istota
creatures (creature) stworzenie, istota
cries (cry) wołać, płakać; okrzyk
cripple okaleczyć, sparaliżować; kaleka; tandeta, odpad
cruel okrutny
cry wołać, płakać, zapłakać, zawołać; okrzyk
crystal kryształ; krystaliczny
cursed (curse) kląć,

przeklinać; przeklęty
curtain zasłona, kurtyna, kotara
curvature skrzywienie, zagięcie, krzywizna
curve zakrzywić, wyginać; krzywa, wygięcie
curved (curve) zakrzywić, wyginać; krzywa, wygięcie; zakrzywiony
cut ciąć, rozciąć
cylinder walec, cylinder, bęben
cylinders (cylinder) walec, cylinder, bęben
dainty przysmak; delikatny, drobny, filigranowy, pełen gracji, wytworny
damp wilgoć; wilgotny, chłodny, przybity, stłumiony
danger niebezpieczeństwo
dangerous niebezpieczny
dare odważyć się, ośmielić, mieć czelność
daring (dare) odważyć się, ośmielić, mieć czelność; śmiałość, brawura
dark ciemny
date datować; termin, randka, daktyl, data
day dzień
days (day) dzień
deadly śmiercionośny, śmiertelny
death śmierć
debate zastanawiać się nad, rozważać; debata, dyskusja
declares (declare) deklarować, zgłaszać, oświadczyć, oznajmić
deep głęboki
definite określony, sprecyzowany, konkretny
degeneration pogorszenie się, degeneracja, zwyrodnienie
degree stopień
delicacy delikatność, subtelność, czułość
delicate delikatny
depended (depend) zależeć, polegać; zależy
deplorable godny ubolewania, opłakany, żałosny
depth głębokość, głębia, otchłań
descend zejść, zstąpić, schodzić, obniżać; upadek, staczanie się
descent opadać; zejście, schodzenie, pochodzenie, najazd, atak, opadanie, rodowód
describe opisywać
described (describe) opisywać
desperately beznadziejnie, rozpaczliwie
detachable odpinany, ruchomy, do oderwania, zdejmowany
detectives (detective) detektyw
develop rozwijać
devices (device) urządzenie, przyrząd, sposób, sztuczka, plan, pomysł
devotion poświęcenie
devoured (devour) pożreć, pochłonąć, niszczyć, pustoszyć; pożarty
diaphanous przezroczysty, przeświecający
did (do) zrobić
die umierać
died (die) umierać; zmarły
differed (differ) różnić się
difficult trudny
diffuse rozproszony, rozmyty, rozwlekły
dignity godność, powaga, szacunek
dined (dine) obiadować, jeść obiad
dinner obiad
dipped (dip) zanurzać, zniżyć, zanurkować, pikować; krótka kąpiel, obniżenie terenu, spadek, pochylenie
directed (direct) kierować, zarządzać, skierować, reżyserować; ukierunkowany
direction kierunek, wskazówka, instrukcja
dirty brudny
disappearance zanik, zniknięcie
disappeared (disappear) znikać, zgubić się
disaster katastrofa
discomfort niewygoda
discovered (discover) odkryć, odnaleźć; odkryty
disease choroba
disengaged (disengage) rozłączyć, zaprzestać, uwolnić się, uwolnić; wolny

dissolve rozpuścić, zniknąć, rozpłynąć; przenikanie
distance odległość
distant odległy, daleki
distended (distend) rozdąć, wydąć, rozciągnąć; spuchnięty, rozciągnięty
distress zmartwić; rozpacz, ból, niebezpieczeństwo
district dzielnica, obwód
ditch zerwać, puścić, porzucić, pozbyć, wymknąć, rozwalić; rów
dive zanurkować, spaść; skok do wody, nurkowanie, spadanie, lot nurkowy
divine odgadnąć; boski
do robić, zrobić
doctors (doctor) lekarz
document dokument
does (do) robić, zrobić
doing (do) robić, zrobić; czyn, wyczyn, sprawka, lanie
doing up (do up) zapiąć, zasunąć
dome kopuła, nakryty kopułą
done (do) robić, zrobić; gotowy, zrobiony
doubt wątpić; wątpliwość
down na dół
downwards w dół, do dołu, skierowany w dół; zniżkowy
dozen tuzin
dr doktor
dragged (drag) ciągnąć, przeszukać, przeciągnąć, wlec, wciągnąć; nudziarz
dragging (drag) ciągnąć, przeszukać, przeciągnąć, wlec; nudziarz; męczący, wlokący się
draw rysować, szkicować, wyciągnąć, przyciągnąć, ruszać się; rysunek
dreadful okropny, fatalny, straszny, potworny
dreamer marzyciel
dress ubierać; sukienka, strój
dressed (dress) ubierać; sukienka, strój; ubrany
dressing (dress) ubierać; sukienka, strój
drew (draw) rysować, szkicować, wyciągnąć, przyciągnąć, ruszyć
drift podryfować, popłynąć z prądem, unieść; prąd, sens, znoszenie
dripping (drip) przepuszczać, ociekać, kapać; kropla; cieknący, kapiący, przemoknięty, ociekający wodą, deszczowy
drive prowadzić, jechać; napęd
drivel ślinić się, bredzić; brednie
driven (drive) prowadzić, jechać
droning (drone) brzęczeć, buczeć, warczeć; brzęczenie, cedzenie przez zęby
drooping (droop) zwiędnąć; pochylenie, opadnięcie; zwisający, opadający
drop upuścić, zrzucić, opaść, przestać, porzucić, rzucić, podrzucić, usunąć; kropla
dropped (drop) upuścić, zrzucić, opaść, przestać, porzucić
drummed (drum) bębnić, zagrać na bębnie; bęben, bębenek, baryłka, beczka
drunkenness pijaństwo
due należny; z powodu
dull nieciekawy, tępy, nudny, nijaki
dwell zamieszkiwać, przebywać, rezydować; dom, mieszkanie, siedlisko
each każdy
ear ucho
early wcześnie
ears (ear) ucho
earth Ziemia
easier (easy) łatwy, wygodny; łatwiejszy, wygodniejszy
easily z łatwością
east wschód
easy łatwy, wygodny
eccentricity ekscentryczność
eddy zawirować, zafalować; wir
edge krawędź
effect dokonywać, doprowadzać; efekt, skutek
effort wysiłek, staranie
eight osiem
either zarówno
elaborate rozwodzić się; złożony, misterny, wyszukany, opracowany
elastic elastyczny,

rozciągliwy
elephant słoń
elevating (elevate) wynieść, podnieść; mechanizm podniesienia
else inny; jeszcze
employment zatrudnienie
empty pusty
enabled (enable) umożliwiać, pozwalać
enclosed (enclose) otoczyć, mieścić w sobie, załączyć; osłonięty, obudowany
encounter napotykać, spotykać, natykać się, doświadczać, zmierzyć się; spotkanie, potyczka
end kończyć się, zakończyć, skończyć; koniec
endeavour starać się; próba, staranie
engine silnik
engines (engine) silnik
England Anglia
English angielski
enigmatic zagadkowy, enigmatyczny
enlarging (enlarge) powiększyć, zwiększyć, rozwinąć, wzrosnąć, rozszerzyć
enormous ogromny
enough dość
entered (enter) wchodzić, wejść
enters (enter) wchodzić, wejść
entirely całkowicie
entirety całość
envelope pokrywać; koperta, powłoka
epoch epoka
epoch-making epokowy, przełomowy
escape uciekać, unikać, umykać; ucieczka, uciekanie
escort eskortować; eskorta
especially szczególnie
essential niezbędny, istotny, zasadniczy
eternal wieczny, nieustanny
even nawet
evening wieczór
ever zawsze
every każdy
everyone każdy
everything wszystko
evolved (evolve) opracować, ewoluować
exactly dokładnie
examination badanie
examined (examine) zbadać, sprawdzać, przeprowadzić kontrolę, kontrolować
example przykład
exception wyjątek
exhilarated (exhilarate) upoić, wprawić
exist istnieć, egzystować
expanse przestrzeń, powierzchnia, bezmiar
expected (expect) spodziewać się, oczekiwać; spodziewany
expecting (expect) spodziewać się, oczekiwać
experience doświadczać, przeżywać; doświadczenie
expert ekspert; fachowy
experts (expert) ekspert; fachowy
explain tłumaczyć, wyjaśniać
explanations (explanation) wyjaśnienie
exploded (explode) wybuchnąć, obalić, wylecieć, spowodować wybuch
explorer badacz, eksplorator
express wyrażać; ekspresowy, szybki
extending (extend) przedłużyć, wydłużyć, rozciągnąć; przedłużanie, rozciąganie się, rozbudowywanie
extraordinary niezwykły, wyjątkowy
extreme skrajny
extremely niezwykle
eye przygladać się; oko
eyes (eye) przyglądać się; oko
fabric materia, konstrukcja, tkanka, tkanina
face zmierzyć się; twarz, pokrycie
fact fakt
facts (fact) fakt
fade wyblaknąć, spłowieć, zwiędnąć, przeminąć
fade away zanikać
failed (fail) nie udać się, zawieść; przegrany
failure niepowodzenie
faint zasłabnąć, zemdleć; omdlenie; słaby
fairy wróżka, bajka; bajkowy, czarodziejski
fall spadać, opadać,

upadać; spadek; autum - jesień
fallen (fall) spadać, opadać, upadać; upadły
fancies (fancy) wydawać się, przewidywać sukces; upodobanie, urojenie
fancy wydawać się, przewidywać sukces, sądzić, wyobrażać, przypuszczać; upodobanie, urojenie, kaprys; niesamowity
fantastic fantastyczny; fantastycznie
far daleko
farm farma, gospodarstwo rolne
farmer rolnik
farther dalej
fashioned (fashion) kształtować, modelować; moda, styl; stylowy
fast szybki
fastened (fasten) przymocować, zapinać, zamknąć; zasuwka; przymocowany, przybity
faulty wadliwy, błędny
fear bać się, obawiać się; strach
fearless nieustraszony
feel czuć, doświadczać, dotykać; uczucie, wrażenie, atmosfera
feet stopy
fell (fall) spadać, opadać, upadać
fellow człowiek, facet, kolega
fellows (fellow) człowiek, facet, kolega
fever gorączka
few kilka
fewer (few) kilka
field pole, dziedzina
fifteen piętnaście
filled (fill) wypełniać, napełnić; wypełniony
finally wreszcie
find odnaleźć; odkrycie, znalezisko, orzeczenie, werdykt
fine grzywna; cienki, delikatny, lekki, pogodny, dobry
finest (fine) grzywna; cienki, delikatny, lekki, pogodny, dobry; najlepszy
fingers (finger) palec
firm firma; mocny, pewny
first pierwszy
fish ryba; (slang) typ, koleś
five pięć
fixings (fix) naprawić, załatwić, przymocować, ustawiać; ustalenie, urządzenie
flannel flanela, myjka do twarzy
flaps (flap) trzepotać, migotać; klapka
flash migać, błyskać, przemykać; błysk
flat mieszkanie; płaski; płasko
flattened (flatten) spłaszczyć, wyrównać, zgnieść; spłaszczony
flattened out (flatten out) rozpłaszczyć, spłaszczyć
fled (flee) uciekać, umykać, frunąć
fleecy wełniasty
fleet flota, park, konwój; szybki, rączy
flight lot, ucieczka
flights (flight) lot, ucieczka
floating (float) unosić się, pływać, rozchodzić się, dryfować; platforma, boja; niestabilny, zmienny
floor piętro, podłoga
flush poczerwienieć, zarumienić się; rumieniec; dziany, nadziany, pełne dobre humoru, wyrównany, równy, będący na tym samym poziomie
fluttering (flutter) zatrzepotać, pomachać, zamrugać, dygotać, powiewać; trzepot, szelest, kołatanie, drganie; dygotanie, trzepotanie
fly latać, lecieć, uciekać; mucha
flying (fly) latać, lecieć, uciekać; mucha; latający
fog mgła
folds (fold) zaginać, złożyć, składać, owinąć, spleść, zwinąć; marszczenie, fałda
follow iść za, jechać za, podążać za, śledzić
food jedzenie
foot stopa
foot mark stopa wysokości
footpath ścieżka, chodnik
for dla
force zmuszać, wymuszać, narzucać; siła, oddział
forcing (force) zmuszać, wymuszać, narzucać;

zmuszając
foremost główny, przedni; na pozycji lidera; najpierw, czołowo
form formować, zakładać, utworzyć; forma, formularz
formed (form) formować, zakładać, utworzyć; forma, formularz
former były
formidable potężny, ogromny, bardzo trudny
forms (form) formować, zakładać, utworzyć; forma, formularz
forth naprzód, dalej
forty czterdzieści
forward naprzód
forwarded (forward) wysłać dalej; naprzód, do przodu; dalszy
found (find) odnaleźć; odnaleziony, ufundowany
four cztery
fragile kruchy, delikatny, słaby
fragment fragment, kawałek
fragmentary fragmentaryczny, oderwany, okruchowy
frames (frame) obramowywać, okalać, formułować; postura, rama; ramowy
France Francja
friends (friend) przyjaciel, znajomy
fright strach, trwoga
frightened (frighten) przestraszyć kogoś, przerazić kogoś; przerażony
fringing (fringe) okalać, ciągnąć się wzdłuż; grzywka, frędzle; skraj; otoczony, poboczny, skrajny
from od
front z przodu, przed
frozen zamarznięty, mrożony
full pełny
funnel lejek
fury furia
fuselage kadłub
gained (gain) osiągać, zdobywać, zyskiwać; zysk; uzyskany
gale wichura
game gra, zawody
gaped (gape) gapić się, rozwierać się
gas gaz
gathered (gather) zebrać się, zbierać, wnioskować
gathering (gather) zebrać się, zbierać, wnioskować; zbieranie
gauge zmierzyć, policzyć, ocenić; grubość, przekrój, wskaźnik, miernik
gave (give) dawać, podawać, podarować
gelatinous galaretowaty
general generał; ogólny
gentleman pan
gently łagodnie, delikatnie
get otrzymać, dostać;
ghost duch, widmo, cień, odbicie
ghost-like przypominający ducha
girth obwód, obwód w pasie
give dawać, podawać, podarować
glass szkło, kieliszek
glasses (glass) szkło, okulary
glide ślizgać, sunąć, szybować; ślizg, szybowanie
gliding (glide) ślizgać się, sunąć, szybować; szybownictwo
glimmering (glimmer) migotać; migotanie, iskra, płomyk, przebłysk
glorious wspaniały
glue przykleić coś, skleić; klej
glue-like przypominający klej
glutinous kleisty, lepki
gnome krasnal, gnom, bankier
go iść, udać się, odejść, zamierzać
go on kontynuować, trwać, iść do przodu
god bóg
goes (go) iść, udać się, odejść, zamierzać
goes with (go with) pasować, towarzyszyć, dziać się jako skutek czegoś
goggles (goggle) wybałuszyć; gogle, okulary pływackie, okulary ochronne
goggling (goggle) wybałuszyć; gogle, okulary pływackie, okulary ochronne; wyłupiaste
goggling eyes (goggle

eyes) z wybałuszonymi oczami
going (go) iść, udać się, odejść, zamierzać; wyjście, odejście, pójście, robienie czegoś
gold złoto; złota
golden złoty
good dobry
gorgeous wspaniały
got (get) otrzymać, dostać
got down (get down) zasmucać, przygnębiać, zapisywać, schodzić
got in (get in) przychodzić, przyjeżdżać, wsiadać, wchodzić
got off (get off) wysiadać, wychodzić, zdejmować
gown suknia, fartuch, koszula szpitalna, szlafrok
gradient pochyłość, stopień nachylenia, gradient
gradually stopniowo, powoli
gravity ciężkość, ciążenie, powaga, grawitacja
grease nasmarować, posmarować tłuszczem; smar, tłuszcz, łój, maź
greasy tłusty, przetłuszczający się, zatłuszczony
great wspaniały, wielki
greater (great) wspaniały, wielki; wspanialszy, większy
green zielony
grew (grow) rosnąć, wzrosnąć, rozwijać się, stawać się
grey szary
grim ponury, zacięty, nędzny, okrutny
grind siekać, ostrzyć, szlifować; harówka, zgrzytanie
groaned (groan) jęczeć, narzekać, skrzypnąć
growing (grow) rosnąć, wzrosnąć, rozwijać się, stawać się
guide prowadzić, zaprowadzać, oprowadzać; przewodnik
gun pistolet
gusts (gust) podmuch, poryw
gusty porywisty, wietrzny
gyroscopic żyroskopowy
habit nawyk, zwyczaj
hackwork chałtura
had (have) mieć; miałem, miałeś, miał, mieli
hail pochwalić, witać się, zawołać do, krzyknąć, pozdrawiać, zatrzymywać, przywoływać; grad
half pół
halfpenny półpensówka, pół pensa
hand podawać, wręczać; dłoń, ręka
hangars (hangar) hangar
hanging (hang) wisieć, wieszać, powiesić; kotara; wiszące, wywieszone
happened (happen) wydarzyć się, zdarzyć się; wydarzenie
hard ciężko
hardly ledwie
harp harfa
harry nękać, dręczyć; Harry - imię
has (have) mieć, ma
hatred nienawiść
have mieć
having (have) mieć; posiadanie, robienie, doświadczenie
hawk jastrząb
hay zrobić bałagan; siano
haycock kopa siana
hazy mglisty, zamglony, niewyraźny
he on
head kierować się, zmierzać; głowa, umysł, spokój, szef
heap zwalić na kogoś coś, ułożyć, leżeć na kupie; sterta
heard (hear) słyszeć, usłyszeć; zasłyszany, usłyszany
heart serce
heart disease choroba serca
heavens (heaven) niebiosa, niebo
heavier (heavy) ciężki; cięższy
heaviness ciężkość, ogrom
heavy ciężki
hedge wykręcić, wykręcać się; zabezpieczenie, żywopłot
height wzrost, wysokość
heights (height) wzrost, wysokość
held (hold) utrzymać, trzymać, odbywać; uścisk; trzymany
help pomagać; pomoc
her jej
here tutaj

heroic bohaterski, heroiczny
herself siebie, sama, się
hesitate wahać się, zawahać się
hiatus przerwa, luka
hideous szkaradny, ohydny
high wysoki
higher (high) wysoki; wyższy
him jemu, jego
Himalayas (Himalaya) Himalaje
himself sam, się, sobie
his jego
hiss syknąć; syk, syknięcie, szum
homburg kapelusz męski
home dom
hook zaczepiać, zainteresować; hak
hope mieć nadzieję; nadzieja
hoped (hope) mieć nadzieję; nadzieja
hopeless beznadziejny
horrible obrzydliwy, potworny
horror przerażenie, groza
horse koń
hot gorąco
hour godzina
house dom
hovering (hover) wisieć, unosić się w powietrzu, wahać się
how jak, jakże, w jaki sposób
however jednak, jakkolwiek
huge ogromny
human człowiek
humble upokorzyć, poniżyć; skromny, pokorny, pełny pokory
humming (hum) nucić, brzęczeć; brzęczenie, nucenie, śpiewanie pod nosem, brzęczek
hummocks (hummock) wzgórek, pagórek, spiętrzenie lodu
humour humor, nastrój, usposobienie
hundred sto
hundreds (hundred) sto
hung (hang) wisieć, wieszać, powiesić, obić tapetami, wisieć w powietrzu; zawieszony
hung about (hang about) kręcić się, pałętać się
hunter myśliwy, drapieżnik, koń do polowania
hurriedly pośpiesznie
hush uciszyć, wyciszyć, uspokoić; cisza; cicho!
I ja
idea pomysł
ideas (idea) pomysł
if gdyby
imaginative obdarzony wyobraźnią, pomysłowy
imagine wyobrażać sobie
imagined (imagine) wyobrażać sobie; wyobrażony
immeasurably niezmiernie, ogromnie
impending nieuchronnie zbliżający się
implored (implore) błagać, napraszać się
important ważny
impose nałożyć, narzucić
impossible niemożliwy
impression wrażenie, ślad, odcisk
improvements (improvement) poprawa, postęp, ulepszenie
impunity bezkarność
in w
in ink napisany piórem
in turn po kolei, w rezultacie, z kolei
inchoate nieokreślony, niesprecyzowany
inclined (incline) przechylić, skłonić, nachylać, mieć na coś ochotę; zbocze, stok; pochyły, skłonny
including (include) zawierać, obejmować; między innymi; w tym, łącznie z
indeed w rzeczy samej
indication oznaka, wskazówka, przejaw
indicator wskazówka, oznaka, wskaźnik, kierunkowskaz
infinitely nieskończenie
inhabit zamieszkiwać
inhabitable nadający się do zamieszkania
inhaler inhalator
ink pokryć, pokrywać tuszem; atrament, tusz
inland śródlądowy, leżący w głębi lądu, krajowy
inquest dochodzenie
insensibility zamroczenie, niewrażliwość, obojętność
insensible nieprzytomny,

niewrażliwy
inside wewnątrz
instant chwila, moment; nie wymagający gotowania, natychmiastowy; od razu
intellectual intelektualista; intelektualny
intelligence doniesienie, inteligencja
intercept zatrzymywać, przechwycić; punkt przecięcia prostej z osią współrzędnych
interesting (interest) interesować się; zainteresowanie, interes, korzyść; ciekawy
intermittent sporadyczny, przerywany
intermittent fever gorączka przerywana
into w
invent wynaleźć, zmyślać
inventor wynalazca
inwards do wewnątrz
iridescence mienienie się tęczowymi barwami, opalizacja
iridescent mieniący się barwami, opalizujący
iron prasować; żelazo, żelazko; żelazny
is (be) być; jest
it to
its jego
itself samo, sam
jeer wyszydzić, wyśmiać; gwizdy, drwiny
jelly galareta, galaretka
jelly-fish meduza
jerk szarpać, pchać; szarpnięcie, nagły ruch
jerks (jerk) szarpać, pchać; szarpnięcie
jerseys (jersey) sweter, dzianina, dżersej
job praca, zlecenie, obowiązek
joint staw, udziec, złącze, spoina, knajpka; wspólny, złączony, ruchomy
joke żart
journey podróż
joy radość
judge osądzać; sędzia
jungle dżungla
jungles (jungle) dżungla
just właśnie
keep trzymać, zostawać, utrzymywać; opieka, piecza, przechowywanie
ken (know) rozpoznać; znany
kept (keep) trzymać, zostawać, utrzymywać; opieka, piecza, przechowywanie
knew (know) wiedzieć, znać
know wiedzieć, znać
knowledge wiedza
known (know) wiedzieć, znać; znany
labour praca, trud
labourer (labour) praca, trud, siła robocza; pracownik fizyczny, robotnik
land lądować, spadać, znajdować się; ziemia, pole, ląd, kraj
large duży
lash bić, chłostać, mocować, umocować; rzęsa, bicz, bat
lashed (lash) bić, chłostać, mocować, umocować; rzęsa, bicz, bat
last trwać; ostatni
lay kłaść
layers (layer) kłaść, wycieniować, ułożyć; warstwa
learn uczyć się
learned (learn) uczyć się; nauczony, uczony
least najmniej
leathern skórzany
leave wychodzić, opuszczać, odjeżdżać, rezygnować
leaves (leave) wychodzić, opuszczać, odjeżdżać, rezygnować; liść, kartka
led (lead) prowadzić, przewodniczyć
left (leave) wychodzić, opuszczać, odjeżdżać, rezygnować; pozostawiony, zostawiony
legible czytelny
leisurely powolny, spokojny, robiony w wolnym czasie; spokojnie, powolnie
less mniej
lessened (lessen) zmniejszyć, złagodzić, obniżyć, przycichnąć; zmniejszony, osłabiony
let pozwolić; dom do wynajęcia, wynajem
level poziom
lever dźwignia, lewar
lies (lie) leżeć, kłamać, znajdować się; kłamstwo
lieutenant porucznik

life życie
lifting (lift) dźwigać, podnosić; winda
lifting gas gaz do podnoszenie np. hel
light zapalać; światło, znicz; lekki, jasny
like podobać, lubić; tak jak, podobnie
likely prawdopodobne
limbs (limb) kończyna, konar, człon
limit ograniczać; limit
limitations (limitation) ograniczenie, niedoskonałość, słabość
lines (line) podszyć, wyściółkować, napełnić; linia, lina, granica, kolejka, kwestia, rola
linking (link) połączyć; ogniwo
lips (lip) warga, brzeg, krawędź
listened (listen) słuchać, posłuchać
little mało
lived (live) żyć, mieszkać, zamieszkiwać; żywy
loathsome wstrętny
London Londyn
lonely samotny
long długi; długo
look patrzeć, spoglądać, poszukiwać; popatrz
look after opiekować się, pilnować, szukać
look at przyglądać się, patrzeć, spojrzeć na coś
looked (look) patrzeć, spoglądać, poszukiwać, wyglądać
looked at (look at) przyglądać się, patrzeć
looked up (look up) sprawdzać, popatrzeć w górę
loose wypuścić, zgubić, uwolnić; luźny
lost (lose) tracić, stracić, przegrać; zagubiony
lots of (lot of) dużo, wiele
loud głośny; głośno
lovely piękny, śliczny, uroczy
low niski
lower (low) niski; niższy
lying (lie) leżeć, kłamać; kłamstwo; kłamliwy, łgarski, leżący
macabre makabryczny
machine maszyna
made (make) robić, produkować, powodować; zrobiony
magnificent wspaniały
mail wysyłać; poczta
main główny
majority większość, pełnoletność
make robić, produkować, powodować
make matters worse co gorsza, na domiar złego
making (make) robić, produkować, powodować; robota, tworzenie, zrobienie, stworzenie
mammalian należący do gromady ssaków
man człowiek
manifestation oznaka, przejaw, objaw
manner sposób, maniera
manuscript rękopis
many wiele
map mapa
margin margines, różnica, przewaga, marża, brzeg
mark oznaczyć, znakować; znak
marked (mark) oznaczyć, znakować; wyraźny, wybitny
markedly wyraźnie
mass masa, tłum, msza; masowy
master opanować; mistrz, pan, kapitan, gospodarz
material materiał
Mathew Mateusz
matter materia, sprawa, problem
mauve fioletoworóżowy
may móc; maj
maybe być może
me mnie, mi
meadow łąka
meant (mean) oznaczać, mieć na myśli; znaczenie, sens, średnia; złośliwy, wredny
mechanic mechanik, rzemieślnik; mechaniczny
mechanism mechanizm
men (man) mężczyzna
merciless bezlitosny
merely zaledwie, jedynie, tylko
merging (merge) połączyć, zmieszać
merging in (merge in) wtapiać się
merit zasłużyć się; wartość, zaleta
mess bałagan, nieporządek, mesa, kantyna
met (meet) spotykać,

natrafiać; spotkanie, poznawanie
method metoda
midday południe; południowy
might mógłby, móc; moc, potęga, siła
mighty potężny
mile mila
miles (mile) mila
mind przejmować się; umysł
mine kopać; kopalnia, mina; mój, moje
minute minuta, sprawozdanie, protokół
minutes (minute) minuta, sprawozdanie, protokół
mischief krzywda, figlarność, intryga, nieszczęście
miserable przygnębiony, nieszczęśliwy, nędzny
misfiring (misfire) nie wypalić, nie zapalić
misshapen zniekształcony
missing (miss) zgubić, tęsknić, chybić, nie trafić; brakujący, zaginiony
mist zamglić; zamglenie, mgła
mistress dama, kochanka, nauczycielka, guwernantka, pani domu, pani
model prezentować, zaprezentować, modelować; model
modern nowoczesny
moment moment, za chwilę
momentarily na chwilę, wkrótce, na moment
monoplane jednopłat, jednopłatowiec
monster potwór, monstrum; gigantyczny
monsters (monster) potwór, monstrum; gigantyczny
monstrous potworny, ogromny, monstrualny
moods (mood) nastrój, humor, atmosfera
morbid niezdrowy, chorobliwy, przesadny
more bardziej, więcej
morning poranek, dzień dobry
mortal śmiertelnik; śmiertelny
most najbardziej, większość
motor silnik
mountains (mountain) góra; górski
mouth usta
mouthed (mouth) usta
moved (move) przenosić, przesuwać, ruszać się; wzruszony
moving (move) przenosić, przesuwać, ruszać się; w ruchu; poruszający
mr pan, proszę pana
much dużo, wiele
much more dużo bardziej
must musieć
my mój
myrtle mirt
myself się, sam, ja sam
mysteries tajemnice, zagadki
mystery tajemnica, zagadka
name nazywać; nazwa
nameless bezimienny, nieokreślony
names (name) nazywać; nazwa
napping (nap) pękać, drzemać, kłapnąć zębami
narrate opowiadać; być narratorem
narrative narracja, relacja
nature natura
nausea mdłości, nudności
near blisko
nearing (near) blisko
nearly prawie
neatly schludnie, starannie, porządnie
necessarily koniecznie
need potrzebować, wymagać; potrzeba
needle drażnić, dokuczać; igła, drut, szpilka, wskazówka
neighbours (neighbour) sąsiadować; sąsiad, bliźni
neither ani
nettles (nettle) parzyć; pokrzywa zwyczajna
never nigdy
nevertheless niemniej jednak
new nowy
newspaper gazeta
next następny
nine dziewięć
nineteen dziewiętnaście
no nie
no wonder nic dziwnego
nobody nikt
noiseless bezgłośny
none żaden
nose ostrożnie

wprowadzić, węszyć; nos
not nie
note zauważyć, wspomnieć, notować; notatka, banknot
note-book notatnik
nothing nic, drobnostka, zero
now teraz
numerous liczny
obliterated (obliterate) zrównać z ziemią, usunąć, skasować, zatrzeć; zatarty
obscured (obscure) przesłaniać, ukrywać; niejasny, niewyraźny
observation obserwacja
obvious oczywisty
occasion okazja, sposobność
occasional okolicznościowy, sporadyczny
o'clock o godzinie
of z, ze
off poza
office biuro, gabinet
oil olej
old stary
on na
once pewnego razu
one jeden
oneself się; sobie, samemu; siebie; samotnie
only tylko
open otworzyć, otwierać; otwarty
opening (open) otworzyć, otwierać; otwarcie, sposobność, początek; otwarty
opinions (opinion) opinia, zdanie
or lub
or so mniej więcej, około
order zamawiać, rozkazać, porządkować; zamówienie, kolejność, rozkaz
organic organiczny, naturalny, jednolity
organism organizm
organization organizacja
original oryginalny
other inny
others (other) inny
our nasz
ours (our) nasz
out na zewnątrz
out of action niepracujący, wyłączony
outer (out) na zewnątrz
outline przedstawić w zarysie; zarys, szkic, kontur
outside na zewnątrz
over nad, ponad, na, w dół
overalls (overall) kitel, fartuch, kombinezon
overmastering opanowanie
overtaken dogonić; wyprzedzony, zaskakiwany
own własny
oxygen tlen; tlenowy
pace przemierzać; tempo, szybkość, krok
paces (pace) przemierzać; tempo, szybkość, krok
padded (pad) cicho stąpać, zawyżać; blok, bloczek, podkładka; wywatowany
page strona
pages (page) strona
paid (pay) płacić, opłacać; płatny, zapłacony
pain boleć; trudy, ból
painful bolesny, przykry
pair para
pale blednąć; blady
paper papier, artykuł, dokument tożsamości
papers (paper) papier, artykuł, dokument tożsamości
parachute zrzucić, dokonać, skoczyć; spadochron
part rozdzielać, rozłączać, rozstawiać; część
particular szczegół; szczególny
passed (pass) przechodzić, mijać, spędzić; przepustka, karnet, przełęcz, przejście
passing (pass) przechodzić, mijać, spędzić; przepustka, karnet, przełęcz, przejście; przechodzący, chwilowy
past przeszłość; po, za, dalej, koło, obok, poza
patch łatać; łata, przepaska, grządka, bruzda, skrawek
pea groch, ziarnko grochu
pea-shooter broń o małym kalibrze, rurka do strzelania grochem
peculiar dziwny, osobliwy, szczególny
pencil ołówek
perceived (perceive) odebrać w pewien sposób, postrzegać, spostrzec;

postrzegane
perfect idealny
perfection doskonałość, perfekcja
perfectly doskonale
perhaps może
peril zagrożenie, niebezpieczeństwo
permanent stały, trwały
perpendicular prostopadły, pionowy
perpendicularly prostopadle, pionowo
person osoba
personality osobowość, charakter, postać
perverted (pervert) deprawować; zboczeniec; zboczony, wypaczony; przewrotny
petrol benzyna
phenomenon zjawisko, fenomen
physical fizyczny
physically fizycznie
picked (pick) wybierać, dobierać, zrywać; wybrany, doborowy
picked up (pick up) podnosić, odebrać, zabrać, nauczyć się
picture obraz, zdjęcie, rysunek
pieces (piece) kawałek
pilots (pilot) pilot
pink goździk; różowy; w świetnej formie
pipe grać na piszczałce, śpiewać, szczebiotać; rura, fajka, piszczałka
pique wzbudzić; uraza, irytacja
place umieścić, położyć, postawić; miejsce
plain równina; zwyczajny, jasny, nieładna, gładki, wyraźny; wyraźnie
plan planować; planowanie, plan
plane samolot, płaszczyzna, hebel
planes (plane) samolot, płaszczyzna
planet planeta
plates (plate) talerz, tabliczka
please prosić, dogadzać, satysfakcjonować, zadowalać kogoś, uważać, życzyć sobie, cieszyć
plenty obfitość; dużo
plotters (plotter) intrygant, ploter
plug wtyczka, zatyczka, korek, prymka
pockets (pocket) kieszeń
poet poeta
point wskazać, wskazywać, celować, wskazywać palcem; punkt
poor ubogi
possible możliwy
possibly możliwie
pounce skakać, rzucić się
poured (pour) nalewać, zalewać, lać
power siła, władza, moc, kontrola
practical praktyczny, realny
pray modlić się, błagać, prosić
precarious niebezpieczny, niepewny
preceded (precede) poprzedzać, iść przed; poprzedzone
precision precyzja
prefacing (preface) poprzedzić przedmową: wstęp, przedmowa
prefer woleć, preferować
premonition przeczucie
present zaprezentować, podarować, przedstawiać; obecny
presently obecnie, niebawem
preserved (preserve) ochraniać, zabezpieczać, zachować; zachowane
preserves (preserve) ochraniać, zabezpieczać, zachować; konserwa, domena, specjalność
pressure nacisk, ciśnienie
presuming (presume) sądzić, założyć, przyjmować, nadużywać
prevailing (prevail) przetrwać, wygrywać, panować; dominujący
prey być łupem dla kogoś, polować na; ofiara
principle zasada
private prywatny
probable prawdopodobny
probably prawdopodobnie
progression rozwój, postępy, poprawa
projection przewidywanie, wizja, projekcja, wypustka, występ
pronounced (pronounce) wymawiać, oświadczać, ogłaszać; wyraźny

proof uodparniać; dowód
propeller śmigło, śruba napędowa
prove okazać się, dowodzić, udowadniać
proved (prove) okazać się, dowodzić, udowadniać; okazały, udowadniany
puffs (puff) dyszeć, sapać, wypuścić dym, pierdnąć; dmuchnięcia, podmuchy, bufka
pulsated (pulsate) pulsować; bijący, walący, pulsujący
pump pompować; pompa
puncture przebić, przekłuć, obalić, pęknąć; przebicie, dziura, nakłucie
pure czysty, niewinny, całkowity
purple poczerwienieć; fioletowy
purplish o zabarwieniu purpurowym, fioletowawy
purr mruczeć; warkot
purring (purr) mruczeć; warkot
pursuit pogoń, dążenie, pościg
put położyć, postawić, kłaść
put forward przesunąć wskazówkę do przodu, zmienić czas na późniejszy, przedstawić coś, wysuwać
qualifications (qualification) dyplom, kwalifikacje, kompetencje
quarter apartament, kwatera, jedna czwarta, ćwiartka, kwadrans, dzielnica, część miasta
queer dziwny; dziwnie
question pytać, przepytywać; pytanie
quick szybki; szybko
quite całkiem
race ścigać się, pędzić; wyścig, rasa
racket robić harmider; rakieta, rakietka, wrzawa
ragged (rag) nabijać się, dokuczać; szmata, gazeta; wystrzępiony, poszarpany, umęczony
rain deszcz
raised (raise) wznosić, podnosić, podwyższać; wzniesiony, uniesiony
rang (ring) dźwięczeć, dzwonić
rapidly szybko
rarefaction rozrzedzenie
rarefied rozrzedzony, ekskluzywny
rather raczej
Raymond Rajmund
reach osiągać, uzyskiwać, dosięgnąć, dojechać, dotrzeć
reached (reach) osiągać, uzyskiwać, dosięgnąć, dojechać, dotrzeć
reader czytelnik
readjust poprawić, wyregulować, dostosować
ready gotowy
real rzeczywisty, realny, prawdziwy
really naprawdę
reason powód, przyczyna
reckoned (reckon) myśleć, sądzić, przypuszczać, liczyć
recognized (recognize) rozpoznać, postrzegać; uznany, autoryzowany
record notować, nagrywać; rekord, nagranie
recovered (recover) wyzdrowieć, wrócić do zdrowia, odzyskać
refusing (refuse) odmawiać; odpadki
regular regularny
reinforce popierać, wzmocnić, umocnić, zwiększyć
relics (relic) relikt, pozostałość
remains (remain) pozostać, nie zmienić się; szczątki, pozostałości
remarkable znakomity, godny uwagi, niezwykły
remarking (remark) zauważyć, komentować, napomknąć; uwaga
remember pamiętać, przypomnieć sobie
reminded (remind) przypominać
report donosić, informować; raport
reproduces (reproduce) wykonać, reprodukować, rozmnażać się, powielać
reputation reputacja
resembling (resemble) przypominać
rest odpoczywać, wypoczywać; odpoczynek
restricted ograniczony, wyznaczony, poufny, tajny, dozwolony od 17 lat
results (result) wynikać;

wynik
retiring (retire) przejść na emeryturę, kłaść się spać, wycofywać się, opuszczać; odchodzący na emeryturę, małomówny
return wracać, powracać, oddawać, odbijać; powrót
revealing (reveal) ujawnić; odsłaniający
revolution rewolucja, obrót
Rheims Reims
rhythm rytm
right wyrównać; prawidłowy, odpowiedni; dokładnie, dobrze
ring dźwięczeć, dzwonić; pierścień, kółko
ring up dzwonić, telefonować
rise wstawać, rosnąć, wstać z martwych, wschodzić; wzrost
rising (rise) wstawać, rosnąć, wstać z martwych; wzrost, wschodzący
risk ryzyko
river rzeka
rivet nitować, przykuć; nit
rotary rondo; obrotowy, rotacyjny
round mecz, runda; okrągły, dookoła
rubbish śmieci, odpadki, bzdury
rudder ster
rudder-bar drążek steru
rule rządzić; reguła; zazwyczaj
run biegać; bieganie, działanie; ciągły
running (run) biegać; bieganie, działanie; ciągły
running on (run on) działać na coś, kontynuować
safe bezpieczny
safely bezpiecznie
safety bezpieczeństwo
said (say) mówić, powiedzieć
sails (sail) żaglować, wyruszać w podróż; żagiel
same taki sam, identyczny
sang (sing) śpiewać
sanity zdrowie psychiczne, zdrowy rozsądek
satisfy zadowolać, satysfakcjonować
saw piła
say mówić, powiedzieć
saying (say) mówić, powiedzieć; powiedzenie, porzekadło
says (say) mówić, powiedzieć; mówi
scale wdrapać się; skala, łuska; wagowy
scamped (scamp) łobuz, przekręt
scared (scare) wystraszyć, spłoszyć, bać się; strach, popłoch, panika; wystraszony, przerażony
school szkoła
science nauka
scribbled (scribble) nabazgrać, nagryzmolić
scum szumowina, męt, kożuch, osad brudu
sea morze
searching (search) poszukiwać; poszukiwanie; badawczy, dociekliwy, wnikliwy, dokładny
seat mieścić, posadzić; siedzenie
second sekunda; drugi, kolejny
see widzieć, zobaczyć, dowiedzieć się; widzenie, wzrok
seeing (see) widzieć, zobaczyć, dowiedzieć się; widzenie, wzrok; ponieważ, widząc że
seem wydawać się, zdawać się
seemed (seem) wydawać się, zdawać się
seen (see) widzieć, zobaczyć, dowiedzieć się; widzenie, wzrok; widziany
semi pół
semi-solid pół stały
sending (send) wysyłać, posłać; wysłanie
sense czuć, wyczuwać; odczucie, zmysł, sens
senses (sense) czuć, wyczuwać; odczucie, zmysł, sens, rozsądek, rozum
separated (separate) oddzielać; rozdzielony
September wrzesień
serious poważny
serpent wąż
serpent-like przypominający węża
serpents (serpent) wąż
served (serve) podawać, serwować, służyć, obsługiwać
service serwisować; usługa, obsługa, praca

set umieścić, postawić, usytuować; zestaw
seven siedem
seventy siedemdziesiąt
several kilka
severe poważny, ciężki, srogi, surowy
shades (shade) osłaniać od światła; odcień, cień
shadow cień; ocieniony
shadowed (shadow) cień; ocieniony
shadowy zaciemniony, ciemny
shaken (shake) zatrząść, potrząsać, wstrząsać; wstrząs; wstrząśnięty
shall powinien
shape kształtować; kształt, forma, w kształcie
shaped (shape) kształtować; kształt, forma, w kształcie
sharp ostry, bystry
shattered (shatter) rozbijać, niszczyć; zrujnowany, roztrzaskany
she ona; używane też w odniesieniu do kraju, statku lub pojazdu
sheet szot, arkusz, tafla, prześcieradło, pościel
shimmered (shimmer) mienić się, drgać; migotanie, blask
shining (shine) świecić, błyszczeć, polerować
shivering (shiver) zadrżeć, zatrząść się, roztrzaskać, dygotać; drżenie, dreszcze, ciarki
shock zaszokować; szok, wstrząs
shooting (shoot) strzelać, pędzić, wystrzelić, rzucać; pęd; spadający, przeszywający, kłujący
shorn (shear) ostrzyc, wystrzyc
shot pędzić, przerywać, strzelać; strzał, wystrzał, rzut
shot-gun strzelba
should powinien
shoulders (shoulder) ramię
shouted (shout) krzyczeć; krzyk, pokrzykiwania
show pokazywać, okazywać, pojawić się, prezentować; widowisko, pokaz
showed (show) pokazywać, okazywać, pojawić się, prezentować; widowisko
shrugging (shrug) wzruszyć; wzruszenie ramion; wzruszając ramionami
side strona, część, bok, krawędź
side-slip ślizg
sideways (sideway) bokami, bokiem; na boki, do boku, z ukosa
sight dostrzegać; wzrok, widok
silencers (silencer) tłumik
silly głupi
silver srebro; srebrny
similar podobny
since od
singing (sing) śpiewać; śpiew, śpiewanie, gwizdanie; rozśpiewany
single pojedynczy
singular wybitny, szczególny, osobliwy, pojedynczy, niezwykły
sinister złowieszczy, złowrogi
sinking (sink) tonąć, opadać, wyciszać; zlew
sinking into (sink into) zatopić w czymś coś
sinuous kręty, wijący się
situation sytuacja
six sześć
size dopasować; rozmiar
skids (skid) wpaść, popędzać kogoś; poślizg, dźwignia
skimmed (skim) usuwać z powierzchni, musnąć, przebiegać; przebiec wzrokiem
skimming (skim) usuwać z powierzchni, musnąć, przebiegac wzrokiem, prześlizgiwać się; przebiegający wzrokiem
skirts (skirt) omijać, unikać, okrążać; spódnica
sky niebo
slacken zwalniać, zmniejszać prędkość, poluźnić
slide zsunąć się, poślizgnąć się; slajd, ramka, ślizganie się
slight urazić; niewielki, drobny
slimy oślizgły, mulisty, mazisty, lepki, oślizły, obleśny
slip wślizgnąć się, poślizgnąć
slippers (slipper) kapeć,

pantofelek, pantofel
slow powolny
slower (slow) powolny; powolniejszy
slowly powoli
sluggish niemrawy, spowolniony, wolny, wolno płynący
small mały
smile uśmiechać się; uśmiech
smoke palić, dymić; palenie, dym
smooth wygładzać; gładki
smoothed (smooth) wygładzać; gładki; wygładzony
smothered (smother) udusić, zdławić, tłamsić, zarzucać, pokryć; zdławiony
smudge rozmazać; plama
snakes (snake) wąż
snap warknąć, stracić panowanie nad sobą, pękać; trzask, pstryknięcie, kłapnięcie, fotka, zdjęcie, kawał, żart, energia, wątek
so więc
soaked (soak) namoczyć; namaczanie; przemoczony, zmoknięty, nasączony
soap mydło
soap-bubble bańka mydlana
soared (soar) unosić się, wzrosnąć, podskoczyć, gwałtownie wzrastać, szybować
soaring (soar) unosić się, wzrosnąć, podskoczyć; wznoszenie, latanie, zwyżka, rośnięcie
sob zaszlochać, łkać; szloch
society społeczeństwo
socks (sock) skarpeta
solid solidny, powściągliwy, beznamiętny, stały, ciągły; lite
solidity twardość, solidność, trwałość, zasadność
solitude samotność
some trochę
somebody ktoś
something coś; bardzo, strasznie
sometimes czasami
somewhat nieco
somewhere gdzieś
soon wkrótce
sopped (sop) rozmoczyć; rozmoczony kawałek chleba, symboliczny gest
sound brzmieć; dźwięk
sounded (sound) brzmieć; dźwięk
sources (source) źródło, początek
south południe
spaces (space) przestrzeń
sparking (spark) iskra
sparking-plugs świeca zapłonowa
speed prędkość
spent (spend) wydawać, spędzać; wydatek; wydany
spiral wzrosnąć; spirala; spiralny
spoken (speak) mówić, przemawiać; mówiony
spot miejsce, plama
spume pienić się; piana
spun (spin) wirować, sięgać, prząść; bomba, rewelacja
squadron eskadra, szwadron, dywizjon
square plac, kwadrat, nudziarz, kąt prosty; kwadratowy
square acre akr kwadratowy
squeak piszczeć, kwiczeć, skrzypnąć, zgrzytać, popiskiwać; pisk
squeal zawyć z bólu, zakwiczeć; kwik, pisk
stains (stain) poplamić; plama
stands (stand) stać, znieść; stoisko, stojak, podstawka, pozycja, trwanie; poważanie
started (start) zacząć, startować, rozpocząć, zrywać się; początek, zryw, wzdrygnięcie; rozpoczęty
stately okazały, majestatyczny
statement oświadczenie
stays (stay) zostać, pozostać, mieszkać; gorset, linka, podpora
steadiers (steady) regularny, stały, jednostajny; mocniejszy
steadily uspokajać; równomiernie, miarowo, stale, pewnie
steady podtrzymać, podpierać; stały, zrównoważony, opanowany
steam para; parowy

steepest (steep) namoczyć, pozwolić; stromy; najbardziej stromy
sticky lepki, kleisty, ciekawski, wścibski, paskudny
stifling (stifle) dusić, udaremnić, tłumić, spowalniać; duszny
still nadal
stillness bezruch, spokój, cisza
stone kamień
store magazynować, przechowywać, gromadzić; sklep, zapasy; duża ilość
storm atakować, pieklić się; burza
story opowieść, historia, fabuła, piętro
straggling (straggle) ociągać się, wlec się; rozproszony, rosnący w różnych kierunkach
straight prosty; prosto
strain nadwyrężać, odsączać; odmiana, szczep, obciążenie, wysiłek
stranded (strand) kosmyk; pozostawiony, unieruchomiony
strange dziwny
stratum warstwa
streamer serpentyna, wstęga
strings (string) nawlekać, zawieszać; sznurek, szereg, struna
strong silny
struck (strike) strajkować, uderzać, spaść, zaatakować, krzesać, wybijać; strajk, uderzenie; powalony
strut kroczyć dumnie; rozpórka
subside ustępować, opadać
substance substancja, istota
substantiate poprzeć, potwierdzić
succession dziedziczenie, sukcesja; ciąg, szereg, seria
successive kolejny
such taki
sudden nagły
suddenly nagle
suffered (suffer) ponieść szkodę, cierpieć, ucierpieć, znosić
summer lato
summit szczyt, na szczycie
sun słońce
sunlight światło słoneczne
superior przełożony; ponadprzeciętny, wybitny, lepszy
supply dostarczać, zaopatrywać; dostawa, zapas
support wspierać; wsparcie
supreme najwyższy, największa
surely pewno, z pewnością
surface powierzchnia
surroundings (surround) otaczać; otoczenie, okolica
suspended (suspend) przerywać, zawieszać; zawieszony, wstrzymany
swallow połknąć, przełknąć; jaskółka, łyk
swallowed up (swallow up) wchłaniać
swayed (sway) chwiać się, kołysać, skłaniać się; wpływ, władza
sweep zamiatać, zamieść, porywać, pędzić, omiatać; szeroki ruch, zakres, kominiarz
sweetly mile, słodko, ślicznie, gładko
swift jerzyk; szybki, błyskawiczny
swiftly prędko
swirled (swirl) kłębić się, zamierzać; zawijas, wirowanie
swirling (swirl) kłębić się; wirowanie, kłębienie się, obracanie
switched (switch) zmienić, przenieść, przesunąć; zmiana, włącznik, rózga, witka
switched on (switch on) włączać
symptoms (symptom) objaw, przejaw
tack przyczepić; gwóźdź z dużą główką
tail śledzić kogoś; ogon, kita, część końcowa, poła
take brać, wziąć, zabrać, podjąć
taken (take) brać, wziąć, zabrać, podjąć; zajęty
talc talk
tale opowieść, historia, baśń
talk rozmawiać, mówić,

opowiadać; rozmowa
tank czołg, zbiornik, cysterna, basen, bak
taste smakować, skosztować; smak, gust
teal kolor niebieski z odcieniem zielonkawym, cyraneczka
tears (tear) łzawić, pędzić, rozdzierać, szarpać się; rozdarcie, łza
telescope teleskop, luneta
tell powiedzieć, wskazać, kazać
ten dziesięć
tender czuły, delikatny, wrażliwy
tentacle macka, czułek, włosek
tentacles (tentacle) macka, czułek, włosek
tenuous cienki, wątły, słaby, naciągnięty, subtelny, luźny
terrible straszny, okropny
terrific olbrzymi, wielki, straszny
terrors (terror) terror
test testować; test, sprawdzian
texture konsystencja, struktura
than niż
that że
their ich
them im
then następnie
theory teoria
there tam
thermometer termometr
these te
they oni, one
thick gruby, gęsty
thin przerzedzać; chudy, cieńki, słaby
thing rzecz
things (thing) rzecz
think myśleć; opinie, myślenie
thinking (think) myśleć; opinie, myślenie
thinking of (think of) myśleć o
thinned (thin) przerzedzać; chudy, cieński, słaby
third trzeci
thirty trzydzieści
this to
those (that) że, te, tamten
though chociaż
thought myśl
thoughts (thought) myśl
thousand tysiąc
threatened (threaten) grozić, straszyć
threatening (threaten) grozić, straszyć; groźny
three trzy
throated (throat) gardło; gardłowy
throttled (throttle) udusić, zdławić; przepustnica, zawór dławiący
through przez
throw wyrzucić, rzucić
throw out wyrzucić, pozbyć się, odrzucić
throwing (throw) wyrzucić, rzucić, niedbale położyć; rzucanie
Thursday czwartek
tiger tygrys
tigers (tiger) tygrys
tilt przechylać, przekrzywiać, przechylać się; nachylenie, plandeka
time czas
times (time) czas
tins (tin) puszka, cyna, blacha
tints (tint) odcień, szampon koloryzujący, koloryzować
to do
to the point na temat, do rzeczy
together razem
tomorrow jutro
too także
took (take) brać, wziąć, zabrać, podjąć
top wierzchołek, szczyt, top
topped (top) przewyższać, przebijać; wierzchołek, szczyt, top, wierzch
tore (tear) łzawić, pędzić, oderwać, drzeć, pędzić, wyszarpać, rozdzierać, rwać; rozdarcie, łza
torn (tear) łzawić, pędzić; rozdarcie, łza; rozdarty
touch dotykać, urazić, poruszać; dotyk
tourbillon (franc.) wir, trąba powietrzna
trace namierzać, wyśledzić, śledzić; ślad, uprzęż
tragic tragiczny
trail podążyć, snuć się, ciągnąć za sobą; szlak, smuga, ślad, trop
transparent przezroczysty, klarowny
travel podróżować, jechać; podróż

trembled (tremble) zadrżeć, drżeć, trząść się
tremendous olbrzymi, ogromny, potężny
trouble niepokoić, kłopotać, zmartwić; kłopot
true prawdziwy
trying (try) próbować, usiłować; próbując, męczący
turn obracać się, skręcać, kręcić się
turned (turn) obracać się, skręcać, kręcić się
turned to (turn to) zwracać się, skierować się, zmieniać się w coś, zmieniać się
twelve dwanaście
twenty dwadzieścia
twice dwa razy
twisted (twist) skręcić; skręcony
twisting (twist) skręcić, kręcić; skręcony, kręty
two dwa
unbroken nieprzerwany
unclouded bezchmurne
under pod
undertaken (undertake) podjąć się
undertaken (undertake) podjąć się, przedsięwziąć; przedsięwzięcie
undoubtedly niewątpliwie
undue nadmierny, zbytni
unexpected niespodziewany, nieoczekiwany
unfortunate niefortunny, nieszczęśliwy
unfortunately niestety
unknown nieznany
unprecedented bezprecedensowy, niespotykany
unquestioned bezsprzeczny, niekwestionowany
unreliable niesolidny, niepewny, niemiarodajny
unscrewed (unscrew) odkręcać; odkręcony
unselfish niesamolubny, bezinteresowny
unsolved nierozwiązany, niewyjaśniony
unsurpassed niezrównany
until aż do
up w górę
up to date aktualny, najświeższy
upon na
upper górny
upward w górę, do góry; zwrócony ku górze
upwards (upward) w górę, do góry; zwrócony ku górze
us nas, nam, nami
use posługiwać się, używać, zużywać; zastosowanie, użytek
used (use) posługiwać się, używać, zużywać; zastosowanie, użytek; używany
vacuum odkurzyć; próżnia, pustka, odkurzacz
vague mętny, niejednoznaczny, nieokreślony, niepewny, niejasny
vainglorious chełpliwy, próżny
valued (value) cenić, wyceniać; wartość; drogi, cenny; ceniony
vanished (vanish) wyparować, zniknąć, pierzchnąć; znikający
vapour mgła, para, opary
vapours (vapour) mgła, para, opary
vast ogromny
veined (vein) żyła, nerw, ton, nuta; żylasty, żyłkowany
veins (vein) żyła, nerw, ton, nuta
velocity prędkość
venetian-blind żaluzja
Veroner Werończyk
verrier (franc.) szklarz, podstawka pod kieliszek
very bardzo
vibrating (vibrate) wprawić, drgać, drżeć
victim ofiara
victorious zwycięski
view patrzeć, postrzegać; widok, zdanie, opinia
village wioska
viscid lepki, zawiesisty
vision wzrok, wyobraźnia, dalekowzroczność, wizja
visit odwiedzać, zwiedzać, oglądać
visitor gość, turysta
visits (visit) odwiedzać, zwiedzać, oglądać; wizyta
void próżnia, otchłań; pusty
vol tom
vol-plane lecicec lotem

ślizgowym; lot ślizgowy
vulture sęp
waist talia, pas
waiting (wait) czekać, oczekiwać; czekanie; oczekujący, czychający
want chcieć, potrzebować
wants (want) chcieć, potrzebować
warm podgrzewać, ogrzewać, ogrzać; ciepły
warning (warn) ostrzegać, upominać, uprzedzać; ostrzeżenie
was (be) być
was after (be after) poszukiwać, gonić, ścigać
wasted (waste) marnować; marnotrawstwo, odpady; zmarnowany, wycieńczony
watch oglądać, obserwować; czuwanie, straż, zegarek
watching (watch) oglądać, obserwować; czuwanie, straż, zegarek
wave falować, machać; fala
way sposób, droga
we my
weak słaby
wealth bogactwo, dobrobyt
weapon broń
weapons (weapon) broń
weather pogoda
weight obciążać, przemawiać
well studnia, szyb; dobrze
went (go) iść, jechać, pójść
were (be) być
west zachód
westward na zachód; zachodni
wet zmoczyć; mokry
whale wieloryb
what co
whatever cokolwiek
when gdy, kiedy
where gdzie
which który
whiff wciągać ustami; zapach, woń, zapowiedź, dmuchnięcie, zaciągnięcie się
while podczas gdy
whip smagnąć, ściągnąć, uderzać, ubijać, ukraść, zrzucać, zabrać; bat, bicz, pejcz
whir brzęczeć; brzęczenie
whirled (whirl) kręcić się, wirować, wiercić się; wir; krótka podróż
whirlpool wir
whirls (whirl) kręcić się, wirować, wiercić się; wir
whisked (whisk) ubijać, szybko zabrać, przeszyć powietrze, śmignąć; trzepaczka do jajek; pacnięty
whistling (whistle) gwizdać, śmignąć; gwizdek, gwizd
white biały
whizzed (whizz) brzęczeć, świszczeć, przebiec
who kto
whole cały
whose którego
why czemu, dlaczego
wide szeroki
will będzie, może, czy; testament, wola
wind wiać, przewijać, pozbawić tchu; wiatr
wind down rozluźnić się, zrelaksować
wing polecieć, poszybować; skrzydło
wings (wing) polecieć, poszybować; skrzydło
wish życzyć sobie, chcieć; życzenie
wished (wish) życzyć sobie, chcieć, życzyć
wisps (wisp) kosmyk, wiązka, smuga
with z
within w ciągu
without bez, spokojnie, bez przeszkód
wonder zastanawiać się, zdumieć się; cud, zdumienie
wonderful cudowny, wspaniały
wondering (wonder) zastanawiać się, zdumieć się; cud
wood drewno, las
woodwork stolarka, stolarki, stolarstwa, konstrukcja drewniana
word słowo
work pracować, działać; praca
working (work) pracować, działać; praca
world świat
worse (bad) źle; gorzej
worst (bad) źle; najgorzej
worth wartość; warty
would (will) będzie, może,

czy
wreath wieniec, kłęby
wreaths (wreath) wieniec, kłęby
wrench szarpnąć, wyrwać; klucz francuski, szarpnięcie
wretched (wretch) nieszczęśnik, nikczemnik; lichy, godny pożałowania
write pisać
writhing (writhe) zwinąć, skręcić; wijący się
written (write) pisać; pisemny
year rok
years (year) rok
yes tak
yet jeszcze
you ty, wy
yourself siebie
youth młodość
zone strefa
zoologist zoolog

Wydawnictwo [ze słownikiem] wydało następujące tytuły:

Wydania angielskie ze słownikiem:

4.50 From Paddington (4.50 z Paddington)
A Christmas Carol (Opowieść Wigilijna)
A Study in Scarlet (Studium w szkarłacie)
A Tale of Two Cities (Opowieść o dwóch miastach)
Alices's Adventures in Wonderland (Alicja w Krainie Czarów)
Anne of Green Gables (Ania z Zielonego Wzgórza)
Around the World in Eighty Days (W 80 dni dookoła świata)
Death on the Nile (Śmierć na Nilu)
Dracula (Drakula)
Forbidden Fruit (Zakazany owoc)
Frankenstein (Frankenstein)
Grimm's Fairy Tales (Baśnie Braci Grimm)
Gulliver's Travels (Podróże Guliwera)
Journey to the Centre of the Earth (Podróż do wnętrza Ziemi)
Memoirs Of Fanny Hill (Pamiętniki Fanny Hill)
Memoirs of Sherlock Holmes (Wspomnienia Sherlocka Holmesa)
Metamorphosis (Przemiana)
Mrs. Dalloway (Mrs. Dalloway)
Murder on the Orient Express (Morderstwo w Orient Expressie)
Peter Pan (Piotruś Pan)
Pollyanna (Pollyanna)
Pride and Prejudice (Duma i uprzedzenie)
Strange Case of Dr. Jekyll and Mr Hyde (Doktor Jekyll i Pan Hyde)
The Adventures of Pinocchio (Pinokio)
The Adventures of Sherlock Holmes (Przygody Sherlocka Holmesa)
The Great Gatsby (Wielki Gatsby)
The Grey Woman and Other Tales (Szara dama i inne opowiadania)
The Horror of the Heights (Groza na wysokości)
The Hound of the Baskervilles (Pies Baskerville'ów)
The House and The Brain (Dom i umysł)
The Invisible Man (Niewidzialny człowiek)
The Jungle Book (Księga dżungli)
The Life and Adventures of Robinson Crusoe (Robinson Crusoe)
The Picture of Dorian Gray (Portret Doriana Graya)

The Prince and the Pauper (Książę i Żebrak)

The Secret Garden (Tajemniczy ogród)

The Sign of Four (Znak czterech)

The Snow Queen (Królowa Śniegu)

The Story of Doctor Dolittle (Doktor Dolittle i jego zwierzęta)

The Time Machine (Wehikuł czasu)

The War of the Worlds (Wojna światów)

The Wonderful Wizard of Oz (Czarnoksiężnik z krainy Oz)

Three Men in a Boat (To Say Nothing of the Dog) (Trzech panów w łódce (nie licząc psa)

Through the Looking-Glass (Alicja po drugiej stronie lustra)

Treasure Island (Wyspa skarbów)

Venus in Furs (Wenus w futrze)

Zen habits (Nawyki Zen)

Wydania francuskie ze słownikiem:

La dame aux camelias (Dama kameliowa)

Le Petit Prince (Mały Książę)

Le Tour du Monde en 80 Jours (W 80 dni dookoła świata)

Les Aventures d'Alice au pays des merveilles (Alicja w Krainie Czarów)

Madame Bovary (Pani Bovary)

Wydania rosyjskie ze słownikiem:

Мастер и Маргарита (Mistrz i Małgorzata)

Русские народные сказки (Rosyjskie narodowe bajki)

Wydania hiszpańskie ze słownikiem:

Alicia En El País De Las Maravillas (Alicja w Krainie Czarów)

Cuentos de Grimm(Baśnie Braci Grimm)

El Gran Gatsby (Wielki Gatsby)

La Reina de las Nieves (Królowa Śniegu)

La Vuelta Al Mundo En 80 Días (W 80 dni dookoła świata)

Las Aventuras De Sherlock Holmes (Przygody Sherlocka Holmesa)

Misericordia (Misericordia)

Wydania włoskie ze słownikiem:

Cuore (Serce)

Le avventure di Alice nel Paese delle Meraviglie (Alicja w Krainie Czarów)

Le avventure di Pinocchio (Pinokio)

Wydania niemieckie ze słownikiem:

Alice's Abenteuer im Wunderland (Alicja w Krainie Czarów)

Die Märchen von Gebrüder Grimm (Baśnie braci Grimm)

Die Schneekönigin (Królowa Śniegu)

Effi Briest (Effi Briest)

Reise nach dem Mittelpunkt der Erde (Podróż do wnętrza Ziemi)

Reise um die Erde in 80 Tagen (W 80 dni dookola świata)

Fiszki:

Angielski Matura Poziom Podstawowy cz.1

Angielski Matura Poziom Podstawowy cz.2

Angielski Matura Poziom Rozszerzony

Słowniki:

Dictionnaire francais-polonais des mots frequents (Francusko-polski słownik frekwencyjny)

Das Deutsch-Polnische Frequenzwörterbuch (Niemiecko-polski słownik frekwencyjny)

Diccionario de las palabras frecuentes español-polaco (Hiszpańsko-polski słownik frekwencyjny)

Dizionario di frequenza italiano-polacco (Włosko-polski słownik frekwencyjny)

Российско-польский часточный словарь (Rosyjsko-polski słownik frekwencyjny)

English-Polish Frequent Dictionary (Angielsko-polski słownik frekwencyjny)

www.zeslownikiem.pl